The Dark Worlds of Joe Pawlowski

THE REVIEWS ARE IN

In the Heart of the Garden Is a Tomb

"It is unquestionably one of the most engaging collections of short stories that I have encountered in the last five years."—M. Grant Kellermeyer, author, editor and blogger

"The author wields his words like a finely-sharpened blade; every word – indeed every detail – adds another layer of mystery and suspense. In short, not a word is wasted."—Ellie Mitchell, Goodreads Review

"Pawlowski does an amazing job building his characters and ensuring that every MC is his/her own person. They have their own backstory, personality, and way of speaking that he brings to life on the page."—Nikki Mitchell, The Book Dragon Blog

The Vermilion Book of the Macabre

"Joe Pawlowski is an artist. With words as his medium, he paints his dark tales so realistically you will have nightmares. This book is a 'must read' if you enjoy the macabre." — Barbara Taylor, Amazon reviewer

"There are dark beings on the outer edges of this fictional world that often make themselves known in particularly gruesome ways. There are demons and witches and little people with peculiar powers and they all add to the appeal of this collection of stories."—Dave B., Amazon Reviewer

"If you love horror then I definitely recommend reading these stories. You won't be disappointed."—Heather Bane, Goodreads Reviewer

"Just have to say: I bought it this week and I love it. Scary and beautiful." — Emanuel Mayer, Facebook

"Ranging from stories of evil curses, unfortunate circumstances, and harrowing monsters Pawlowski unravels a narrative where the characters are the anchor point, the setting is undisputed, and the darkness of these stories settles uncomfortably in the mind of the reader." — Blogger and YouTube personality Gloria McNeely

The Cannibal Gardener
"A quick and gory read with a surprise ending I did not see coming," —Irene Cole *Worth a Read* website

"An exciting tale of terror to the very end."—Shelly Neinast, Goodreads Reviewer

"Fans of James Rollins will love this author. I can't wait to get started on his other books!"—Ashley Dunn, Goodreads Reviewer

"The ending comes with a twist you don't see coming."—Sterling Kirkland, Goodreads Reviewer

"This is an interesting book that takes the reader on a twisted journey through the minds of some warped people." — Amazon Reviewer

Why All the Skulls Are Grinning
"Sinister, unexpected endings kept me on the edge of my seat and left me with my mouth hanging open."— Theresa Bourke, Brainerd Dispatch.

"*Why All the Skulls Are Grinning* ended up being a fantastic read for me who generally does not read or watch the horror genre. The short stories were descriptive and drew you into the story so you could picture where you were, who you were with and what they may be thinking. Being caught up in storytelling, I found many of the endings were a surprise but made sense with the masterful way the story was weaved. I would say Joe honored his craft by successfully scaring the hell out of me with a couple of nightmares especially after reading 'Alien Eggs' and 'Uncle Morven!' — Tammy Severe, Amazon Reviewer

"Chilling, curiosity-invoking, and at times downright creepy."— Kelsey Hawley, Rochester Post Bulletin.

Dark House of Dreams

"The story had me drawn in from the start. The book is well-written and creepy. — Heather Bane, Goodreads

"The story line caught my attention at the very beginning and kept me interested throughout the entire book." — Jeanne Richardson, Amazon Reviewer

The Watchful Dead

"Pawlowski possesses the talents of a classic great writer, and this reader found myself pulled to the page as 12-year-old Ring Gargery experiences loss, brutality, friendship, and love. Behind the dark title lies a spellbinding, outstanding story. I suspect — and hope — we'll hear more of Pawlowski's Ring Gargery tales!" — Lissa Carlson, Wisconsin editor/publisher

"In the city of Hastur, Ring's family are slavers, but his father and uncle have loftier ambitions. Political ambitions, which they hope to attain by some fairly sneaky, roundabout methods involving pirates and a captured island witch with the power to awaken the dead. ... All in all, it's a gutsy, ambitious, skillful exploration of cosmic/epic dark fantasy that brings something new to both facets of the genres." — *The Horror Review*

Best wishes!
Joe Pawlowski

Echoes From a Shoreless Void

Joe Pawlowski

Glint Media

NEW HOPE, MINNESOTA

Also by Joe Pawlowski

The Watchful Dead
Dark House of Dreams
The Vermilion Book of the Macabre
The Cannibal Gardener
Why All the Skulls Are Grinning
In the Heart of the Garden Is a Tomb

Joe Pawlowski/Glint Media
New Hope, Minnesota
www.joepawlowskiauthor.com

Publisher's note: This is a work of fiction. Names, characters, places, and incidents are a product of the author's imagination. Locales and public names are sometimes used for atmospheric purposes. Any resemblance to actual people, living or dead, or to businesses, companies, events, institutions, or locales is completely coincidental.

Book layout © 2017 BookDesignTemplates.Com
Book cover by SelfPubBookCovers.Com

***Echoes From a Shoreless Void*/Joe Pawlowski**
1st edition
ISBN: 979-8-9857407-4-5

For Keith Peterson

"I see the terrifying spaces of the universe enclosing me, and I find myself attached to one corner of this expanse without knowing why I have been placed here rather than there, or why the life allotted me should be assigned to this moment [rather] than to another in all the eternity that preceded and will follow me. I see only infinity on every side, enclosing me like an atom or a shadow that vanishes in an instant."

—Blaise Pascal, *Thoughts, Letters and Minor Works*

Contents

Prelude

I t's your last day of vacation, and you've decided to buy yourself a little something to remind you of this scenic Minnesota burg. Perhaps a T-shirt or a mug emblazoned with the town's name. Some artifact to remind you in the coming depths of your tiresome workdays that you have been somewhere and seen something beyond the confines of the tiny life you've built for yourself.

It's late afternoon, and the stores on Main Street feature in their windows charming displays of assorted souvenirs, knickknacks, and gewgaws. There are statuettes of wide-eyed waifs, risqué plaques, posters, pennants, colorful clocks, commemorative plates, collectors' spoons and thimbles, ashtrays, and salt shakers, but nothing catches your fancy.

Down a side street, you spot a bookseller's shop. It's dusty and neglected-looking, but something about it calls to you. A sign reads SECONDHAND TOMES, which strikes you as an oddly archaic name. Curiosity piqued, you decide to enter.

As you pass through the well-worn door, a bell chimes, and a tall, slender man with a goiter on his neck steps from some back room to the counter and spreads his hands on the counter's surface. "Good day," he says, studying you.

You reply in kind, and begin browsing the musty shelves. All the while, you feel the bookseller's somber eyes on your back, but you try not to let it bother you.

After fifteen minutes, you've made your selection: a storybook from your youth, back when your parents told you that you could be anything, and you believed them. You hand the book to the gaunt salesman, and he pushes another volume across the counter toward you.

"What's this?" you ask.

"It's the book you came for."

"How do you know what I came for?"

"Trust me. I have a knack for this."

"For what?"

"For sensing what a customer truly wants." He smiles, but it's a cheerless grin.

When you touch the book's surface and run a finger down its spine, you feel a slight chill. You try to read the title on the cover, but the letters have so faded as to become illegible. You start to open the book, but the salesman gently stops you with one slender hand.

"You'll want to spend some time perusing this one," he says.

Rather than argue, you buy the book, without further examining it, and the storybook you previously selected, and the bell rings again as you step toward the sidewalk. Looking back, you see the man with the goiter watching you intently, the cheerless grin still on his face.

Little Dogs

"Truth and the dream were so mingled that now he could not divide
one from the other."
—Arthur Machen, *The Hill of Dreams*

The white man went down hard, smacking the back of his head on the icy sidewalk with enough force to produce a resounding crack. The sound of the fall drew the attention of gangly Latino teen Michael Santiago.

This was two weeks before Christmas, some years before the world trembled in the shadow of the Covid pandemic. Before people started wearing facemasks and keeping each other at arm's length. It happened in the morning on Bass Lake Road in New Hope, Minnesota, near the CVS Pharmacy. To be honest, when Mikey first approached him, he figured the odds were fifty-fifty that the white man was dead.

The fellow had been walking a pair of little dogs, a miniature pinscher and a moppy mutt that looked part Japanese chin. The dogs were licking their owner's face but were getting no response. Middle-aged and clean-shaven with a jutting lantern jaw and eyebrows that resembled iron filings, he appeared thoroughly drained of blood. If he was breathing, it wasn't with enough vigor to lift his chest or issue fog from his nostrils into the biting December air.

"Hey, man, are you okay?" Mikey asked, touching the man's shoulder with a caution reserved for handling the dead. The two dogs

3

barked at Mikey, but he ignored them. "Come on, man. Wake up. Do you need an ambulance?"

The prone fellow groaned, then coughed. His eyelids opened but his eyes just rolled around in his head. This spooked Mikey, who stepped back and dialed 911 on his cell phone. "Yeah, there's a guy over here on Bass Lake Road, near Winnetka. He needs a doctor."

Mikey waited for the ambulance, holding the dogs by their leashes. The moppy one already took a liking to Mikey, milling around one of his legs and looking up to be petted. The miniature pinscher quit barking but still growled at him.

When the emergency technicians arrived, a sizable crowd had gathered around Mikey, the dogs, and the groaning man.

A squad car pulled up behind the ambulance. A cop got out and asked Mikey a few questions while the EMTs loaded the white man onto a board and lifted him into the ambulance. The cop chewed on a toothpick.

"Just slipped on the ice, huh?" the cop said, eyes tensing as they studied Mikey in a way that made the teen uneasy. Then the cop walked off, writing on a little notepad. He asked a few others in the crowd if they'd seen anything, but they hadn't.

The cop and the EMTs then climbed back into their vehicles and drove off, the ambulance's lights flashing, siren wailing. Members of the crowd, muttering to one another, drifted apart to resume the activities they had been pursuing before the ruckus with the fallen white man had diverted them. For his part, Mikey stood on the icy sidewalk of Bass Lake Road, realizing he still had two little dogs by their leashes.

He bent down and looked at the moppy one's collar. He found a pair of silver tags. The first one reported the recent date of the dog's latest rabies shot. The second was heart-shaped and bore the dog's name—Abu—and an address on Gettysburg Avenue North. It was near Liberty Park, maybe a ten-minute walk from where Mikey was, which wasn't that far, but the cold was already turning Mikey's hands to frozen claws, and his arms and legs were chilled clear through to the bone.

Abu didn't seem to mind the cold, but the miniature pinscher shivered.

"Alright," he said. "I guess I'm taking you two home. Come on. Let's go."

At least it was a sunny day, though that didn't help much with the temperature. Especially not with the traffic whipping the wind into frigid gusts. Maybe two inches of snow flattened adjacent yards, with rabbit and squirrel tracks cutting through stretches of powdery smoothness. Christmas lights and holiday statuary were ubiquitous.

They trudged a few blocks, down to where Gettysburg Avenue joined up with Bass Lake Road, then followed Gettysburg to Liberty Park. Just beyond it, they came to a mouse-gray, one-story ranch house with cedar-shake siding and an attached garage. They walked up to the front door, past a frosty likeness of St. Nicholas, and Mikey rang the doorbell. He waited a few seconds, then rang it again.

Nothing. Nobody home. Mikey peered through the door glass but saw only darkness inside. He double-checked the address on Abu's tag to ensure he had the right place, but, of course, he did.

"Damn." He eyed the two little dogs, who looked back at him, awaiting directions.

There was no way in the house or the garage without breaking something. It was too cold to leave them outside. (Who knew when the owner would show up?) He guessed he'd have to take them home with him and try back again later.

Mikey lived with his older cousin, Carlos, on 60th Avenue, another ten-minute walk from the house on Gettysburg. He didn't relish the idea of showing up at Carlos' with two stray dogs, but what choice did he have?

Luckily, Carlos was in a good mood. Mikey had fetched him two packs of Kools from the gas station where a girl they knew worked, and Carlos, who'd been out of smokes since late last night, was more than eager to thumb a pack open. Shirtless, in flannel pajama bottoms, he worked away the cellophane and shook out a butt. Lean, buff, and heavily tattooed, Carlos' good looks were marred by a deep scar on his face. When people asked him how he got the scar, he'd reply, "You should see the other guy."

"What's with the dogs?" he said evenly, lighting up.

Mikey told him the story of the collapsed man and the ambulance and the cop and the mouse-gray abode on Gettysburg. Carlos nodded, blowing smoke rings over Mikey's head. He looked like he'd just woken up, but that didn't mean anything. Carlos always looked that way.

Carlos drew a great lungful of smoke and talked while holding it in. "Any messes, you clean it up." He let the smoke out. "And I want them out of here by tonight. If they're still here in the morning, I'm calling the dogcatcher."

Mikey agreed. What else could he do? Carlos' house, Carlos' rules. Not that there were many regulations involved in living there. His cousin had promised Mikey's parents that their son would go to school, so there was that rule. And housemates were expected to chip in what they could for expenses and food. Otherwise, the boy was free to come and go as he pleased.

He shared a room and a bunk bed with a towering, beefy Hawaiian called Tiny. If Tiny ever gave up lawlessness as a pastime, he could maybe take up Sumo wrestling. Six-foot-six, just this side of three-hundred pounds, with dense, curly hair, the big fellow had an easygoing disposition generally, but he could be an ugly drunk.

Tiny was on parole for attempted carjacking. Luckily, he was only fourteen when it happened and was charged as a minor. He probably wouldn't have done any time, but a gun was involved, so he spent two years in the Red Wing Correctional Facility. Minnesotan Bob Dylan recorded a song about the place, "The Walls of Red Wing," for use on the album *The Freewheelin' Bob Dylan*, but the song never made the cut, and at the time was available only on Dylan bootlegs, though Joan Baez and Rambling Jack Eliot recorded versions of it. Of course, the song was complete fiction. Dylan was never locked up in Red Wing, nor had he even visited the prison.

According to Tiny, the facility wasn't that bad. The food was okay, and people left you alone. Well, anyway, left you alone if you were six-foot-six and just shy of three hundred pounds.

He had this thing about sharks. He sometimes wore a shark's-tooth pendant around his thick neck and had a tattoo of a grinning Great White on his forearm. "One-third of all shark attacks are Great Whites," he said of the image. "It's the world's largest predatory fish. It has three hundred razor-sharp teeth and one of the most powerful bites known to humans. If you ever come across one in the water, you'd better get to land as quickly as you can. Otherwise, you could very well end up as shark chum."

Whenever he gave that spiel, he'd smile broadly, impressed with his own knowledge on the subject. Tiny wasn't the keenest tool in the toolbox, but he knew a thing or two about sharks.

"Where'd you get them dogs?" he asked from the bottom bunk as Mikey and the dogs entered the room. He seemed pretty interested.

Mikey repeated his story. Told him Carlos was only giving him a day to return them to their owners or he was calling animal control.

Tiny sat up, hunched under the top bunk's side rail, and reached out a meaty paw for the miniature pinscher. The dog yapped and nipped at Tiny's fingers, but the big guy didn't seem to mind. "Bet you could get fifty dollars for a dog like this," he said. "Maybe a hundred."

The little dog gave up trying to bite Tiny, and just sort of scowled at him. Tiny fumbled with the dog's tags. "Says his name is Phoenix. What kind of a name is that for a dog?" He held up Phoenix and studied him. "If he was my dog, I'd call him Killer."

Both of the boys laughed at this. Killer. A ridiculous name for such a little dog.

"I figure I'll head back to the house on Gettysburg after lunch. Maybe someone will be around by then."

"Okay if I tag along? I got nothing better to do."

"Sure."

LUNCH WAS A SMORGASBORD of assorted canned foods collected Thursday from the food-shelf pantry in Golden Valley. Canned corn, canned pinto beans, canned carrots. These they meticulously portioned out onto paper plates. Carlos, still shirtless in his flannel pajama bottoms, contributed an extra half a bag of Fritos corn chips from his bedroom stash, and Tiny broke out a sleeve of Ritz crackers.

Mikey had nothing to add, but he figured the owner of the dogs might slip him a few bucks for bringing them home. Maybe enough to get them a frozen pizza or two.

After lunch, the skinny Latino kid and the Sumo-sized Hawaiian tramped with the dogs down 60th Avenue. The plows had come through, shoving piles of snow from the road to the ends of driveways, where homeowners would have to shovel to get their cars out. The boys walked in the street, kicking at errant snow ridges and talking about the girl at the convenience store who sold Mikey the Kools for Carlos.

"Yeah, I know Brandi Castellanos," Tiny said. "She's alright. Smokin' bod, but she's got those weird eyes."

"What do you mean?"

"You know. Spooky eyes. It's always like she can't believe what she's looking at. Like you're the weirdest thing she's ever seen."

Mikey had never noticed this about her but said nothing. He kind of liked her.

Abu paused to pee in the snow.

"And she's a Packers fan." To Tiny, there was no getting around this. He loved the Vikings and absolutely hated the Green Bay Packers. He hated them like he hated them from his old neighborhood, as any Minnesota football fan could understand.

By the time the two came to the mouse-gray home on Gettysburg, a deep chill had set in. They slogged past the frozen St. Nicholas figure to the front door, where Mikey pressed the doorbell. He was about to press it again when the inside door opened.

Peering out at them stood a woman in her fifties, five-three, a hundred and sixty-five pounds, uncombed black hair obviously dyed. She wore slippers, a faded, print dress, and smoked a cigar—not the thin cigarillo-type women sometimes smoked to look cool but an honest-to-gawd, king-size stogie. She chomped on it like Sergeant Rock from the comic books and worked it around her words as she talked. After pointing with an unpolished fingernail to a sign on the screen door that read NO SOLICITORS, she said, "You boys better not be selling anything, or I'll call the cops and have you arrested."

She had the gruff voice of a smoker, and a stink eye of withering intensity.

"No, ma'am," Mikey said. "We're not selling anything, just bringing your dogs back."

She frowned at him. "Dogs?"

"Phoenix and Abu. Their tags have this as their address." He held Phoenix loosely in his arms.

Her face softened. She opened the outer door wide enough to reach out and take Phoenix from Mikey. "Well, I'll be. Okay. You two can come in. But don't get any ideas." An ash from her cigar fell to the floor.

Phoenix barked at her once: a timid, little bark that quickly trailed off to a whine. He looked positively embarrassed, as if he'd been caught by this woman doing something naughty.

The boys followed the woman into her living room, Tiny tugging at Abu's leash. It took a moment for their eyes to adjust somewhat to the murky darkness once the door was closed. Thick fabrics shrouded every window, letting in only bands of light at their edges. A single candle burned at the center of a low coffee table that sat beside a couch covered in clear plastic. Also on the table was a thick, hardcover book entitled *The Names of the Demons*.

The overall effect was funereal, or, at least, put one in mind of a séance. The air, weighted and stuffy, was laced with the smell of the woman's cigars.

On one wall, shelves of old-fashion porcelain dolls leered at them.

She set down Phoenix, who scurried over to Mikey. "Where did you get these dogs?" She motioned for the two young men to sit on the couch, which they did reluctantly. She sat facing them in an overstuffed armchair.

"Mikey found them," Tiny offered, rubbing his hands together.

"I see."

She kicked off her slippers, crossed her legs, and fidgeted a bare foot in and out of a crease of sunlight. When her toenails caught the light, they revealed themselves as claw-like, thick and pointy, and yellow as dried mustard.

"Mikey," she said, taking a pull from her stogie and blowing the smoke into the air, "Where did you find the dogs?"

9

Phoenix growled softly, and Abu cowered beneath an end table. It was almost as if they knew she was talking about them.

Mikey had always been taught to regard anyone who spoke directly to him. This was the polite thing to do. But he was uncomfortable looking at the woman. In fact, he was uncomfortable directing his gaze anywhere in this gloomy room. Finally, he settled on the shelves of dolls. These dolls were ancient, countenanced like ghosts—too small to be considered toddlers really, too large to be considered infants—in frilly dresses and as joyless as the dead, with mournful eyes.

Some of them looked back him. Some stared off into blackness. Mercifully, many were too shadowed to clearly discern.

"On Bass Lake Road." Mikey's mouth was going parched, and he couldn't seem to generate any spit. "This guy fell and passed out."

"The man who was walking them?"

"Yeah. He slipped on the ice. I grabbed the dogs' leashes to keep them from running off."

He glanced at her. She was considering what he said. In the dark, her eyes grew moist and glittery. He looked back at the dolls.

"What happened next?" she said, almost in a whisper.

He cleared his throat. "The ambulance came and took him away." He felt his gaze drawn back to her. Even though he was telling the truth, he felt as if he were lying. Now he struggled to pull his focus away from her.

"But not the dogs." She worked her cigar to the opposite side of her mouth.

His chest tightened. "Not the dogs."

"And when did all this happen?"

"This morning." It was all he could do to get out these two words. He glanced over at Tiny, but the big Hawaiian was no help. Tiny stared open-mouthed, looking more pasty-faced than Mikey had ever seen him.

Realizing she expected him to say more, Mikey sputtered: "I brought them right over. Over here. But no one was home." There was a pleading quality to his voice; he feared she might not believe him.

Clearing his throat once more, he said, "If these dogs aren't yours, why do they have your address on their collars?"

A glass ashtray sat on one arm of the chair, and the woman tapped her ash into it. The cigar tip glowed a menacing red. "I sometimes pick up strays. I keep them for a while, and then I sell them. Phoenix and Abu I sold to a fellow who lives on Boone Avenue. That's probably who you saw fall on the ice. He must not have got around to buying new tags yet."

"Look, we should get going," Mikey said.

"Yeah, going," Tiny piped up.

But neither of them stirred an inch.

Then something moved in the dark, close to the floor at one side of the woman's chair. At first, Mikey thought it was a hallucination. Then there arose a nervous chittering sound.

"There you are, Donald." She leaned over the side of the chair and lifted a mound of fur to one shoulder. "Look who's here. Phoenix and Abu. They've come for a little visit."

It was a squirrel she'd placed on her shoulder. An albino squirrel, maybe a fox squirrel, with a bright white coat and a bristly white tail, perched and *chit-chit-chittering* from the woman's shoulder at Mikey and Tiny and the two dogs.

Mikey had never seen anyone with a pet squirrel before.

"Donald is my husband," she said.

The periphery of the room shrank. Mikey found himself focusing on the woman's glistening eyes—on the diamond chips of mesmerizing sparkles in the shadowy hollows of her ancient skull. It was as if he was witnessing an unfolding revelation that took his breath away.

For several minutes, neither boy broke the silence that had fallen over them.

Finally, the woman said, "You boys deserve some kind of reward. For bringing Phoenix and Abu back to me."

Mikey held up his hands. "Look, you don't owe us anything. We should just go."

He managed to rise shakily to his feet. The woman with the cigar watched him, curious, her foot still bobbing at the knee.

He hurried to the door. "Nice to meet you," he muttered. "C'mon, Tiny."

But Tiny didn't move. He just sat on the couch dumbstruck. Despite his size, in the dimness of the living room, he'd taken on an eerie resemblance to the porcelain dolls on the shelves.

Mikey stepped from the house, letting the screen door slam shut. He expected Tiny to be right behind him, but the big guy wasn't.

Outside, the wind had picked up, making it feel several degrees more frigid than it had been when they'd walked over: too cold to stand around on the street for very long, waiting for Tiny to join him. Mikey considered ringing the bell again and letting Tiny know he was heading back to Carlos', but he just couldn't gather the courage to do it.

Tiny was big enough to take care of himself.

Mikey walked the snowy streets back toward the house on 60th Avenue, past the spot where Abu'd peed and where they'd kicked at the ridge of snow. He wanted to say it was the last time he saw Tiny, but he really couldn't. Not with any conviction anyway.

A WEEK LATER, Mikey met Brandi Castellanos at the Caribou Coffee shop in Crystal, just over the border from New Hope on Bass Lake Road. They sat at a small table near a window that looked out on a sun-blasted parking lot.

Brandi, olive-skinned and narrow-faced, wore a red-and-black quilted jacket over a lavender cardigan, and, okay, one of her eyes was a little cocked but there was nothing spooky about them, as Tiny had claimed. Mikey could always tell what she was focusing on, and, at that moment, she was focusing directly on him.

"So, whatever happened with Tiny?" she asked, poking a plastic straw into some caramel-mocha concoction called a Turtle Cooler. Mikey was going to order an almond latte but decided a hot cocoa sounded more manly.

"All I know is I never saw him walk out of that house on Gettysburg. I mean, he must've, right? But I never saw it. And, as far as I know, I'm the last one to have seen him."

She sipped from her drink. Then she said, "What did Carlos say?"

Mikey shrugged. "Carlos said Tiny always was a little flaky. Who knows?"

"But isn't Tiny on parole?"

"I guess. But so far, his parole officer hasn't called. Maybe Tiny just took off. He sometimes talked about going to Hawaii—'the old country' he called it, though he'd never actually been there before."

"Did he take anything with him?"

"Nah. But he didn't really have much. A few shirts that had seen better days, some comic books, and this shark's-tooth pendant." Mikey extracted the charm from beneath his open coat. Set in silver on a silver chain, the tooth winked in the sunlight. "That's about it."

"Did you ask about him? At that house on Gettysburg?"

Mikey avoided eye contact with her. He didn't want her to see the glint of fear the question had loosed in him. He looked out at the rows of shiny cars parked in the snowy lot. "I haven't been back there since all this happened. I suppose I should go, though."

"I'll go with you."

"Alright."

They finished their drinks and strolled out to Brandi's car.

Besides being sunny, the day's temperature had spiked at around thirty degrees Fahrenheit, which was almost balmy for a December day in Minnesota, especially compared to last week's freeze fest. They passed one guy in the parking lot wearing cargo shorts and a Steely Dan T-shirt. A true Minnesotan.

Brandi drove a 2000 Volvo S70 SE, black with blooms of rust on the side panels and the hood. The car had over a hundred-and-fifty-thousand miles on it, and its muffler was shot, but it got her to work and back and was good enough to chug around town in. And she only paid nine-hundred dollars for it. Well, she only really paid four-fifty, since her roommate, Anna, paid half. Brandi and Anna shared the car.

The Volvo turned left on Bass Lake Road, then hung a right at the stoplight on Gettysburg.

Mikey pointed out the house and Brandi parked on the street in front of it.

The garage gaped open on a carless expanse of cracked concrete. Inside, a pale-looking dude, about Mikey's height, in sunglasses, overalls and a Twins jacket, was rifling through a coffee can of screws and nails.

Just passing through the threshold of the garage gave Mikey an uneasy feeling, but he tried to hide it in front of Brandi. "Excuse me, sir."

His voice startled the guy, who turned around sharply and squinted at the young folks. "Whaddaya want?" His voice was a mixture of surprise and anger.

"We were just wondering if the woman with the little dogs was home."

He studied them for a moment, then grimaced into his can of metal bits. "Whaddaya want with her?" White-haired, buck-toothed and rawboned, the man tried sounding nonchalant, but nervousness crept into his voice.

"We just wanted to ask her a question."

He plucked a one-inch, zinc-plated Philips screw from his can and eyed it. "What kind of question?"

"Well, I came here last week with a friend, and I was just wondering if she knew what happened to him."

This angered the man, and he looked threatened. "Whaddaya mean, 'what happened to him?'"

Mikey glanced at Brandi and saw she wasn't picking up the weird vibe the guy was giving out. "Well, I left before he did, and I thought he might have said something to her. He's been missing for a week now."

The guy frowned melodramatically. "Well, she ain't here, and we don't know nothing about where your friend went."

Mikey was trying to decide what to say next when a yapping poodle burst onto the scene. He wasn't sure where the dog came from. Maybe they had one of those doggy doors that let pets come in and out at will. The dog was a full-sized poodle, big and hefty, with curly black hair.

"Hush up, Ukupanipo!" the man commanded, but the dog got in a few more yaps in spite.

"Uko—" Brandi said.

"Ukupanipo," the dude replied. "It's the name of some Hawaiian shark god, I think. I don't know. My wife names all the dogs around here."

Mikey felt like he'd just been hit with a shovel. "Your wife?"

"That's right." The man set down the coffee can, and put the retrieved screw in the pocket of his Twins jacket. "Anything else?"

Mikey was silent for a moment. Then he said, "Excuse me, but what's your name?"

The dude took off his sunglasses, revealing pink, albino eyes. "Why, it's Donald," he said.

Caveman

"And I said unto him: 'Tell me what it is that is falling out on the Earth that the Earth is in such evil plight and shaken, lest perchance I shall perish with it?'"
—*The Book of Enoch*

T he woods didn't look the same as they had that day. The landscape and the placement of the trees were all wrong. Where the ground should have dipped into a shallow valley, it now leveled off in a weedy plain dotted with sickly-looking pines. The ancient logging trail they'd been following north was replaced by a footpath that veered eastward.

Maybe he just remembered it wrong, but Billy Griggs didn't think so.

It had taken him a year to build the courage to return to this spot in the forest where he and his friends had first awakened on that fateful day in Wash Greavor's Chevy pickup.

Hard to believe it'd been a whole year.

This was the place, though. He knew it by the marks that had somehow survived a year of erosion: the tire marks from the blowout that had left them stranded that night.

When he'd first decided to return to this place, he'd hoped Wash would come along with him, but just the mention of Buena Vista State Forest had brought a look of terror to Wash's eyes. Billy guessed he couldn't blame him. For Wash and him, these woods held powerful memories.

But the way Billy saw it, that day remained an open-ended chapter in his life that deserved at least an attempt at closure.

He recalled stumbling through the door of the beer-can-littered cab of Wash's truck, half asleep and still a little buzzed from the night before, and looking out on the logging trail to where it continued through overgrown grass, wild oats, and lamb's-quarters, cutting down between red oaks and cedars into a valley before ambling up again.

But where was that valley now? Had someone ripped out the old-growth trees and filled in the depression for some reason? He could see plowing over the trail to dissuade future four-wheelers from following that route, but why would they cover up a whole valley?

There'd been nothing about any landscaping at Buena Vista in the news that he could recall.

Billy yanked a backpack from the cargo bed of his Ford F-150 and hitched the sternum straps over his shoulders. He fastened on a water canteen, returned to the cab, and reached under the driver's seat. He slipped out the holster with the Colt Commander, secured it on his hip, and started walking north, now certain that was the right way, logging trail or no logging trail, valley or no valley.

His bearings were seldom mistaken.

Hulking and full-bearded in his red-checkered shirt, Billy felt like a Northwoods lumberjack, a mini-Paul Bunyan. All he needed was an axe and a blue ox, and the illusion would be complete.

That time a year ago, there had been three of them—Wash, Matt Dribbin, and Billy—setting off in this direction through these woods in search of civilization. Matt had been visiting from Gary, South Dakota, and they'd decided to take a ride: drink some beers and do some four-wheeling on Puposki's old logging trails. Billy and Wash hadn't seen Matt for two years, and they figured they were two years overdue for a good time.

They'd ended up in Buena Vista State Park. He remembered rounding Strand Lake in the night, headed easterly, and the next thing he knew, they were four-wheeling through creek beds, up and down hillsides, taking on impossible angles, stereo blasting Ghost and Metallica, the three of them draining can after can of Schmidt beer, and toking from Matt's one-hitter. He remembered Matt laughing as they were jostled about in the cab of Wash's Chevy. Then Wash started laughing, too, and pretty soon, all three of them were howling as the pickup crashed through branches, twigs, and brushwood, leaves slapping loose all around them.

Why couldn't they just have gone bar hopping in Bemidji? He must have asked himself that question a thousand times.

The three of them hadn't gathered in so long, partly due to the pain-in-the-ass Covid-19 pandemic that had shut down unnecessary travel since the previous March, but it also had to do with all the sadness and grief surrounding the death of Matt's dad. Matt needed time to heal, and they didn't know what to say to him anyway, so they'd given him space.

But, really, how could you ever recover from losing your dad that way?

Billy hadn't gone to the funeral. Neither had Wash. For one thing, it was over fifteen-hundred miles from Puposky to Maitland, South Dakota. For another, getting time off work from Home Depot seemed like a hassle, especially since this wasn't a family funeral or anything, and they'd have to miss a few days.

But these were really just surface reasons for not attending.

The deeper one had to do with the way Matt's dad had died: sliced up and partially eaten while at a real-estate convention in Indianapolis by the serial killer known as the Midwest Butcher. Just thinking about it made their skin crawl.

Besides, the maniac was still out there somewhere, maybe even watching the funeral and tracking some of the mourners. *You don't know.* And even if he wasn't, media types would be there, taking pictures to run in newspapers and magazines for everyone to see. Might even be TV cameras.

No, the aura of evil had touched Ben Dribbin and left its smoldering mark on the closed casket where he lay in pieces. Billy and Wash weren't going anywhere near that.

Today was chillier and more overcast than it had been when the three of them set off walking a year ago. The sky teemed with cobwebby, dark clouds, but the TV weatherwoman had promised no rain. Just in case, Billy had packed a rain slicker. By his estimation, meteorologists got it right about fifty percent of the time.

Since there was no trail anymore, Billy had to make his own way, trying to keep as due north as possible, gauging his progress by the placement of the veiled smudge of eerie white that was today's sun. He pushed his way through the weedy plain, past knotweed and

19

marshelder, and wild buckwheat, through a thick rim of paper birch and outlays of box elders and black oak.

He wasn't sure how far it would be to the clearing and the weathered wood house they'd come to that day, but if these were there, they would be his first clear landmarks.

Another mile, maybe?

But after two, Billy feared his memory was jacked. Maybe the shock of what had happened to Matt that day had hopelessly derailed his recollections. Now and then, he'd recognize a sweep of forest in a flash, but then the memory would just as quickly escape him. Aside from these failing glints of recognition (which were more like déjà vu than solid remembrance), nothing along the way looked familiar.

Sure enough, it began to drizzle, so Billy drew the rain slicker from his backpack and pulled it on. He knew he should head back, but there was a stubbornness at his core that goaded him on.

The sprinkle brought vibrancy to the forest, making the greens pop out at him, making the blacks and browns richer; bringing to glistening life the occasional protrusions of limestone and granite. Tiny creatures—a chipmunk, a snowshoe hare, some kind of vole perhaps— waited out the rain patiently under broadleaf plants. From the branch of a jack pine, an owl turned her head in a perfect pivot and blinked at him.

Then he saw it.

Ahead was a footpath that led across a meadow to a mound of crystalline rock and the shadowy mouth of a cave, larger than the one Matt, Wash, and he had come across that day but close enough in appearance to stop him dead in his tracks. The gleam of the forest's vibrancy turned suddenly crisper, and an icy knot formed in his gut. His mind's eye recalled the slinking thing, the slithering thing, shovel-mouthed and fang-toothed, that had emerged from that other outcropping of rock.

He touched the .45 Colt Commander on his hip, reassuring himself that it was still there.

Pushing through the premonitory dread that had taken hold of him, he drifted cautiously down the footpath toward the cave opening.

The drizzle's crinkling sound masked the footsteps approaching Billy from the rear.

"An interloper, eh? A trespasser in Paradise."

The voice, slightly slurred, startled Billy from his thoughts. Turning slowly, he found himself confronted by what he took to be a bum of some kind: a filthy, rag-garbed derelict with a crudely made fur hat, barefooted and holding the two barrels of a shotgun—a firearm that must have been a hundred years old—directly at him. Water dripped from the open barrels.

To say this creature was a representative of humanity would require some stretching of the term. Let's say humanity in its abstract. Every feature, every angle of his being hinted at deformity. One half of his face contorted in a paralytic grimace, and one yellowish brown eye discharged a trickle of pus.

Feeling almost as if he were in a movie, Billy raised his hands. "Look. I'm just a hiker in a state forest. I don't want no trouble with you, friend."

"When thou saw a thief, then thou consented with him; and has been partaker with adulterers." The fellow's greasy hair and beard were too long and tangled to gauge his age accurately, but he must have been at least forty.

The yellow-brown eyes focused past Billy into some hallucinatory distance, and the young man understood at once that this grisly character pointing a shotgun at him was out of his ever-loving mind.

"Listen, mister," he said, "I'll walk back the way I came, get in my truck, and drive away, and you'll never see me again."

"Impious miscreant, disguising your villainies with lies." He cocked the hammer on his gun. "Hear ye not the prayers of the righteous?"

Billy's raised hands began to tremble.

Then louder: "Hear ye not the prayers of the righteous?"

A gasp hitched in Billy's throat. "I do, I do," he said. He fell to his knees, clasped his hands together, and bowed his head. He tried to think of a prayer but couldn't remember any. Finally, he said in a thin little voice that he barely recognized as his own, "I pray the lord my soul to keep." It was the only shred of supplication he could recall. He repeated it, again and again. "I pray the Lord my soul to keep. I pray the Lord my soul to keep."

Through squinting lids, he watched the derelict lower the shotgun and gape at him. He could almost see the wheels turning beneath his assailant's filthy scalp. The yellow-brown eyes narrowed, and the bum scratched his chin, drizzle beading and dripping down his brow.

Finally, he muttered, "He cometh with ten thousand of his holy ones, and the Watchers shall quake with great fear." He thumbed the hammer of the shotgun closed. "All nature fears Him, but not the sinners." Here the bum lifted a finger skyward and repeated, "Not the sinners."

Billy considered bolting. He had the .45 semi-automatic at his side and could maybe draw it before the madman could fire on him. Maybe roll into high weeds for cover. But doing so would take an act of courage he just couldn't muster, try as he might.

Am I just a lowly coward, after all?

It was the sort of epiphany a person hopes never to realize.

Yes, for all his bulk and bluster, those were genuine tears in Billy's eyes, and he couldn't stop shaking. For a minute, he thought he might pass out. He hadn't even the strength to beg for his life.

"Get up," the gunman ordered.

Now Billy's eyes were wide open. He unclasped his hands. It had stopped raining but it looked to start up again at any second. He rocked back to his feet and rose, the knees of his jeans soaked clear through.

"Can I go?" That thin voice of cowardice again.

The crazed gunman lifted his barrels toward the cave. "Follow the path."

"Look, can't I just go?" He was jiggling now to keep from loosening his bladder.

"The path. Move."

The derelict motioned with the shotgun again, and Billy moved.

He had to duck to get through the mouth of the cave. Inside, the smell of piss and sweat and wormy soil nearly overpowered him. He kept his head down to avoid bumping it against the smoke-stained ceiling.

A dying campfire in the center of the chamber threw off sufficient light that, as his eyes adjusted, he could see well enough. A rumpled bedroll and a half-dozen religious books lay beside the fire. A hodgepodge of used cups and saucers gathered to one side, along with open-topped Mason jars of wild blueberries and a tall glass jug of water. In other areas lay a heap of animal hides, a toolbox, scraps of cloth, fragments of treated wood, pieces of leather, stacked kindling, and assorted dross no doubt largely discarded by campers and hikers, and other visitors to Buena Vista State Forest.

From a peg hung a parka that might have been a leftover from World War II. A bucket near the entranceway served as a poor man's urinal.

"Listen, I have some money," Billy said.

"Is that what you behold, a lover of money?"

"Well, you look like you could use a helping hand."

"Kneel!" the madman commanded.

Billy knelt.

First, the derelict removed Billy's rain slicker, then he pulled the Colt Commander from its holster at Billy's hip and set it aside. Then, from the leather scraps, cord lengths were plucked and used to bind Billy around the chest and back, pinning his arms to his side.

"Sit!"

Billy sat in the dirt next to the fire. "Listen, if I go missing, I have friends who'll come looking for me." The sound of his own voice scraped a nerve. He shuddered at its whiney tone.

"Let them. Then, the last times will come upon them, as well. And, with their final breaths, they shall become reverent and learn to fear the long-suffering God."

Billy felt warmth spread at the joining of his legs. *Christ, I've pissed myself!*

Get a handle on things, Billy, before this lunatic gets it in his head to shoot you.

"You live here, mister?" He struggled to calm his voice.

"Since aught-one," the madman said, drawing up across the fire from Billy and settling on the bedroll. "The way of darkness is crooked and full of cursing." He laid the gun on the ground beside him, picked up one of the religious books, and flipped it at Billy.

Lost Books of the Bible, it was titled. A badly worn paperback edition, dog-eared and filthy, it had on its cover a wood carving of

23

fiendish-looking angels being cast to Earth. Over the title, stamped slightly at an angle in faded lavender was the legend: PROPERTY OF ST. PETER REGIONAL TREATMENT CENTER.

"It's all in there if you'd care to look." He backhanded pus from his weeping eye. "When they put me in that cage, I was on the dark path of idolatry, of pride and hypocrisy and double-mindedness. I was covetous and arrogant, and deceitful. Just like you. Just like all the others. Then my eyes opened to the truth."

Billy swallowed. "I'd like to know the truth. But my arms are tied, and I can't open the book to read it."

The lunatic rose, picking up the shotgun and carrying it to where Billy sat. Was this nutcase actually going to untie his hands? Billy looked up just in time to see the stock of the ancient scattergun coming down at him. He reeled from the shock of the blow and tumbled into unconsciousness.

WHEN HE AWOKE, night had fallen. Through the open cave doorway, a million stars and a half-moon lit the sky and the meadow and silhouetted a clumped topiary of paper birch, spindly pines, and fat cedars. Now he was tightly bound at the arms and the legs with assorted thicknesses of leather cords that left him feeling almost mummified. Sticky blood had coagulated at the side of his head from where the maniac had struck him. The wound throbbed.

He looked around for the Colt Commander, but there was no sign of it. Nor was there any sign of his captor.

He tried moving around like a worm but it was painfully slow and difficult. Rolling wasn't much of an option, given he only had so much room to roll around in. If he could stand, maybe he could just hop away. Sitting up was no problem, but standing without using his hands was a real challenge. Several attempts resulted in his being pitched to the ground, smacking his face on soil and grit.

He was making the umpteenth effort when he sensed a presence at the cave opening.

He twisted his neck and saw the madman in the fur hat watching him, a squirrel carcass dangling from the end of a stick. "Thought you might be hungry," the derelict said, stepping over Billy and approaching the fire.

Squatting, he pulled a fixed-blade hunting knife from among the rags he wore and, with expert precision, relieved the squirrel of all skin. He tossed the bloody skin onto his collection of hides. Then he forced the stick he'd been carrying into the squirrel's denuded skull and far down his throat.

The carcass now sizzled over the open fire.

"I'm not feeling very hungry," Billy said on his belly, watching as the flames licked the squirrel's tendons and gristle.

"You'll eat. The fruitful Earth yields its food plentifully in due season both to man and beast, and to all animals that are upon it, according to His will."

Billy quit trying to roll or sit or rise to his feet. Hopelessness washed over him.

In his mind, he ran through the events that led him to his current untenable situation. From that night a year ago when the tire blew on Wash's pickup. To the next morning when the three of them had set off through the woods, following an old logging trail they thought would lead to safety. Past the collapsed wreckage of the old house, half fallen over with rot, and into the ancient graveyard with its sunken mounds and wooden markers. And then, on to ... Cat's Back Ridge. That's what the sign had called it: the crystalline rock formation that looked roughly like the back of a tailless cat. At its base, of course, lay the wedge of shadow from which his every nightmare since had crawled.

"What's your name?" Billy asked.

At first, the derelict didn't answer, so consumed was he in roasting the crackling flesh. Uncle Buster had once told Billy the aroma and taste of cooked squirrel was indistinguishable from chicken, but this cooking squirrel smelled nothing like chicken to Billy. Instead, it just smelled like death.

"My name is Behemoth, for I occupy with my breast a waste wilderness in the garden where the elect and righteous dwell."

"How long have you lived here, Behemoth?"

"Since I fled the torment of the prison where they confined me." He back-pawed his weeping eye, the smoke seeming to irritate it. "They

25

thought they could fool me by naming the dungeon after a saint. But I could see it was a fearful place. A prison for angels where I would be locked forever."

"But you escaped?"

"Somehow. I recall the paneled wood of the doctor's office, the little vial of pills he handed me. The nurse started screaming, and I remember throwing elbows and fists, crashing down the carpeted corridor. I know I hid for some days with my book in the basement of the old church, drawing water from a rusty pipe. At night, I prowled the building, finding little cakes to eat in the cabinet of the room behind the altar. It wasn't much, but it kept me going."

"This was in St. Peter?"

Behemoth looked up from the braised squirrel. Mention of the name St. Peter had brought a fierceness to the yellow-brown eyes. "I remember finding more books in the church library. Not sure how long I stayed altogether. The next thing I knew, I was breaking down the door of a fishing cabin. *That's* where I found the shotgun!" He looked amazed to have recalled this.

"So, you walked all the way here from St. Peter?" Billy did calculations in his head. "That's like three hundred miles."

"I walked from one place to another place. Sometimes the ground was hard as rock, and sometimes, it was soft. I climbed mountains, lived in the trees, ate mushrooms and berries, and survived day to day. Sometimes I watched them from the branches of the trees: the transgressors, the evil-doers, the deniers of the Lord of the Spirits. I watched them wander around aimlessly, wasting their time in pursuit of things that would only eventually be taken away from them. I walked through their Babylons and saw many transgressors turned into pillars of salt. In the snow and the rain, it didn't matter. I followed the trees and the howling of the wind until I came to this place, which I knew at once was Paradise."

He left the fireside for the stack of plates, selected one, pulled the skewer from the squirrel's throat, then used the fixed-bladed knife to carve the poor creature in half. With the tip of the knife, he scooped out the guts and flung them across the room into the fire. Then, after helping

26

Billy sit up, he sliced off a chunk of meat from one half of the squirrel, held it out on the beveled edge of the shiny steel blade, and said, "Eat."

Billy did.

THAT NIGHT, in his dream, Billy no longer sought to escape the cave but rather crept farther into it, into a damp passage that wound deep underground. The leather straps no longer bound him, and Behemoth, now wearing a black silk mask, led the way, clutching a fiery flambeau.

They wandered through a length of squat stone arcs ornamented with sculptured skulls and welcoming skeletal hands, past scurrying rats, and down a musty stone stairway littered with gnawed bones that appeared to be human but not quite. Then, at the foot of the steps, an enormous grotto, chiseled from limestone, extended well beyond the reach of the torch's light.

Whatever this place was, it was immense: an underworld realm where spacious blackness pressed down on Billy from hugely vaulted ceilings and sections of wall that vanished from sight with every tentative step he took; where the dampness was almost thick enough to lodge in his throat. A place beyond knowing and time and civilization.

They walked through the darkness until it so engulfed them that soon his entire orientation consisted of Behemoth and the flaming brand.

At last, the madman halted and peered into the gloom ahead for an instant. Then he turned, his face eerily phosphorescent in the torch's glow, and waved Billy closer.

"It's what you seek," Behemoth said excitedly in his slurred voice.

He held high his brand and it cast a light on a stone sepulcher, its surface patterned in a tangle of ghoulish forms: frenzied demons dancing promiscuously amid sprawling ruins in a circle of monoliths.

At the sight of it, Billy shivered. "Let's go back."

Behemoth handed him the torch, hurried maniacally to the tomb, and pulled at its stone lid. The rubbing together of stone created a wild squealing that roused a flutter of bats overhead. The lid screeched clear of one corner, and light now shined on an internal crease. The crypt released an odor vile beyond description. It swarmed Billy and hung oppressively in the damp air.

The flambeau's light trembled in his hand. "Let's go, man." That's what Wash said to Matt and him that day when that creature uncoiled at them. "Come *on*." Wash's words exactly, the panicky plea: "Let's go, man!"

But Matt hadn't gone with them that day. Instead, he had just stared dumbstruck as the bug-eyed brute attacked.

Behemoth, veins threatening to burst from his filthy neck, yanked at the lid with both hands, his bare feet leveraged against the crypt's side. The cover slipped a bit more, then a bit more, then ... BOOM! It crashed to the ground, sounding like an explosion echoing into the vast distance.

Behemoth, who had fallen over, now bounced to his feet in triumph, holding an open hand toward the uncovered tomb as if offering it to Billy as a gift.

From the rancid depths of the stone coffin, a figure rose in the torchlight: a wrinkly, desiccated corpse, missing lips and patches of face, exposed muscle juiceless and gray. Eyes, deep-set in their hollows and shriveled, turned toward Billy, paused, then sparkled with recognition.

"Why have you brought me here, Behemoth? What is this?"

Then Billy recognized the T-shirt the dead creature wore. Though faded and moldered and stained with the oily discharge of decomposition, the shirt featured the likeness of a giant mosquito and the legend: MINNESOTA STATE BIRD. The last time he'd seen that shirt was ... Gaping at the corpse's skull, he felt a frigid swirl unleashing inside him.

Lightheaded, he said, "Matt?"

It was Matt, it had to be; Matt Dribbin, his friend and fellow graduate of Bemidji Technical College. Matt, who had stood petrified with fear as the monster approached them that day. As Wash and Billy had scrambled for their lives. Matt, who had been missing for a year in Buena Vista State Forest, was now found buried deep beneath the ground in this place of never-ending night.

Billy turned back to where Behemoth had been standing, but there was no longer any sign of the crazed hermit.

Twirling with the flambeau, he caught a glimpse of movement. He watched and listened intently for what this movement might be, but in his heart, he already *knew*.

Slinking into the torchlight came the snake-thing, black and scaly, with hair on its throat and a noxious-yellow belly. It was as he remembered it: dragon-like in its dimensions; its massive snout, flat and square; its eyes bugged out black and yellow from below a beetling brow. Its forked, black tongue flitted out in Billy's direction. Baby snakes writhed along beside the beast, which had lifted onto its tail, rising six feet off the ground, ready to strike. A new foulness filled the air.

Now he was choking, choking on the dampness and the darkness and the stench that gathered in his gullet. Choking on the fear that seized him. The torch fumbled from his grip as the serpent widened its mouth, baring long and pointy ivory teeth. Its black-and-yellow eyes rolled deliriously in its head.

As he struggled for breath, Billy's eyes snapped open, and he was back in the fire-lit cave, looking up at the sooty ceiling. On his chest, Behemoth sat, pushing down and squeezing Billy's neck, strangling the bound and helpless captive. The cretin's greasy hair dangled in Billy's face.

Billy twisted and writhed, wildly flexing and working what muscles he could. He managed to upend the derelict's fur hat from its crown but Behemoth's hands remained clenched at his throat. Billy bucked and contorted, fighting unconsciousness. His lungs burned from lack of oxygen.

Somehow, he managed to curl completely around till he faced the gritty floor, and he felt the hermit lose balance and tumble in a thud beside him.

His cheek to the soil, Billy huffed and wheezed and snorted the cool, trapped air of the cave, expecting at any minute Behemoth to come back at him for more.

But he didn't.

29

As awareness flooded Billy's tortured frame, he twisted face-up, sat, and looked with fury into the paralytic countenance of the rag-garbed madman. "Why did you do that?" Billy demanded.

Behemoth's filthy fingers twisted the frayed ends of his beard, and he considered Billy as if unsure how to answer the question. As if not knowing himself why he had done it.

He let go of his beard to dab fluid from his weeping eye. "You can't go back. You'll tell them where I am."

"No. I won't. I swear. No one will ever know about you. You have my word."

"They'll put me back in a cage."

"I promise: I won't say anything to anyone."

Behemoth's features hardened. "Keep thy tongue from evil, and thy lips that they speak no guile."

This again. Quoting discarded scripture.

Billy was weighing his reply when the wretch's eyes grew wide, and he bolted across the room to the toolbox. "I don't have to kill him to keep him from talking." He carried the metal box to the fireside, excitedly popped it open, and began rummaging through its contents.

"Behemoth, what are you doing with those tools?"

The madman lifted a pair of silver pliers and held them for Billy to see.

"What do you want with that?"

Instead of answering, Behemoth pulled from his ragged clothing the fixed-bladed hunting knife. He thrust the knife's blade into the fire and held it steady until it began to glow from the heat.

Billy watched with horror. "You're not using that on me, are you?"

Rather than answer, the cave dweller scrambled from the fire, pushed Billy onto his back, and once again sat on his chest, with his filthy knees pressed against Billy's ears. He tapped the hot blade to Billy's lips, which opened reflexively, and forced the pliers into Billy's mouth, clamping onto the edge of his tongue and yanking.

It happened so fast. Billy barely had time to scream.

His tongue stretched rubbery, the tip now a good four inches past his nose. Tears filled his eyes as the length of his tongue lit up with excruciating pain, the root aching brutally but refusing to let loose. He saw the knife flash before his eyes and come down deep in his mouth, searing every surface it came in contact with. Then his neck cracked back, and the smell of burnt flesh filled his nostril, and sickly warmth sept into his mouth.

His severed tongue drooped ashen and bloody from the jaws of the pliers.

Behemoth examined it briefly, then tossed it into the fire.

RED-HOT PAIN robbed Billy of any more sleep that night.

As the hours crawled from night to day, the fiery aching so thoroughly possessed him that he wished Behemoth had taken not just his tongue but his entire head.

His lips, inner cheeks, and the hollow where his tongue had once rested swelled and throbbed relentlessly. His stomach rebelled, though he managed to keep down what little his captor had fed him. Although the maniac had effectively cauterized the wound with the heated knife, rivulets of blood continued to lace Billy's saliva for much of the day, dripping from his puffed lips and down his bearded chin in the form of red-threaded drool.

He spent most of the day in tears, crying not only from his physical suffering but for his loss; for the injustice forced on him that left him irreversibly altered. When he wasn't feeling anguish for having been reduced, he seethed with hatred for the villain who had reduced him.

Late in the day, the pain subsided enough to become bearable. Behemoth left a bowl of water near him from which he could wet his lips. Drinking was trickier now that he was unable to regulate his fluid intake with his tongue. Several times he choked before he developed the knack of using his throat muscles and the tilt of his head in concert.

For his part, Behemoth acted as if nothing unusual had happened. He brought in an armful of dead branches for the fire, collected berries and field mushrooms, and sat in the cave opening with his back to Billy, reading from one of his books, ignoring his injured captive. If there was an ounce of pity or regret in him for what he had affected, he didn't show it.

As Billy's pain eased somewhat, the resulting greater clarity brought with it a supreme urgency: he desperately needed to construct

31

an escape plan. If he didn't, it was anyone's guess what part of him Behemoth would hack off next.

Though the maniac at all times kept the shotgun in view and more or less within reach, he seemed to have all but forgotten the Colt Commander Billy had brought along. Billy suspected Behemoth had hidden the .45 among the collection of rags across the room.

Billy saw this as an opportunity. If he could somehow free his hands from the leather strips that bound him and get ahold of that pistol, then he had a real chance. True, he'd had a similar chance when the madman first approached him in the drizzly field outside the cave. Then, cowardice had prevented him from acting. But that was before Billy understood the full measure of danger Behemoth represented.

Still, Billy wondered whether he'd now have the courage to act decisively. *How deep does that streak of yellow truly run?*

Behemoth mashed some mushrooms and berries at dinnertime, and spoon-fed the mixture to Billy. Eating without a tongue was even trickier than drinking. He'd lost the ability to manipulate food in his mouth when chewing, and swallowing required intense concentration, as choking on solids was more perilous than choking on liquids.

And, of course, his sense of taste had largely become a thing of the past.

Nonetheless, he managed, and the sustenance helped settle his stomach.

HE SPENT MOST OF THE NIGHT restless, drifting in and out of light sleep.

At one point, as the cobwebs of his dreamworld came undone, he emerged to a memory of Uncle Buster taking him horseback riding at the stables just outside Barrytown, Illinois. The place was called the Flying K Ranch, if he remembered correctly. He was about fourteen at the time. He'd selected a chestnut Morgan named Emily, a gentle creature with perky ears and expressive eyes who meandered along at a steady pace next to Uncle Buck's dun mare. It was the perfect day for a ride: early autumn, wheat-color grass, leaf colors just beginning to turn. After about two hours, the dusty trail circled back to the stables, and

Billy felt the mild letdown that comes at the end of a memorable adventure.

Billy and Uncle Buster watched a ranch hand saddling a rust-colored Tennessee Walker in the stables. The worker, a thickset, wavy-haired blonde with freckles, tightened the cinch, then led the horse for several feet and yanked on the cinch again.

"Why'd she tightened the saddle twice?" he asked his uncle.

"Sometimes horses fill their lungs with air to keep the saddle from getting tight. When they let the air out, there's slack on the cinch. If the horse gets away with it, a rider can actually slip off the horse's side. Old-timers used to knee stubborn horses to get the extra air out of their lungs, but these days people walk them a bit, then retighten the cinch. Keeps the horse honest."

Of course!

Billy attempted to expand his chest, but Behemoth's leather strips restricted his movement. The bands bit into his back and arms. Because, when Behemoth had bound him, he had been too complacent, too docile in accepting his fate. But if he puffed out his chest and pulled his arms out slightly from his body when the binds were attached, he'd create slack—perhaps enough to wiggle free. If the madman didn't notice the ruse.

Billy had a chance if he could free his hands and get hold of the Colt Commander.

Behemoth removed the straps thrice a day to allow Billy to go to the bucket near the cave's entrance to answer the calls of nature, keeping the shotgun steady on his captive the whole time. Then he laid out the strips and had Billy lie over them face-down on the ground. He sat on Billy's legs and reknotted the lashes at Billy's back.

The routine had become familiar enough, and Billy wondered whether Behemoth might not be bored with the repetition. For Billy, it represented a reprieve from the tedium of captivity, but for his captor it had perhaps become a tiresome chore.

Billy's mouth was still sore and throbbing and felt stuffed with cotton, but now he had a plan. He drifted back to sleep, reinvigorated with a feeling he'd begun to fear lost to him for all time: hope.

The following day, Behemoth was in a foul mood. He stormed around the cave in a hunched gait, knocking over saucers and plates, kicking through his carefully sorted piles of junk, and whipping wood into the fire hard enough to scatter sparks into the air. Billy tried to mime, "What's the matter?" but the lunatic ignored him, ranting from his profane texts and leaving the cave altogether for extended periods, the shotgun always in tow.

Breakfast time came and went unaddressed—the same thing with lunch. Billy's stomach growled, and he was forced to soil himself due to Behemoth's inattention. The only positive that came from all this was Billy saw a glint of metal among the kicked rags: he was right about where his captor had hidden the Colt Commander!

By early evening, the maniac managed to calm down a bit and crouched between Billy and the fire. He eyed the captive angrily, pawing seepage from his bad eye, and said, "By their desire of gain, betrayers have deceived men, leading them according to the lusts of sinners."

Billy hitched his shoulders as far as the leather binds allowed, leaning his neck to one side and raising his eyebrows—trying to get across to Behemoth that he didn't understand.

"You spoke!" The words ejected like spittle from Behemoth's colorless lips. "Last night. In your sleep. I heard you! You said the snake was coming to get you. That you felt the approach of its dagger-like fangs. The words were unclear but clear enough that I could understand them. Clear enough that anyone could."

The half-frozen face turned beet red. "I cut out your tongue to keep you from talking, but it did no good."

Billy felt new iciness creep through his veins. He'd discovered he could still talk yesterday when his abductor had gone out scrounging for firewood. He judged his vocal ability to be somewhat on par with a half-wit's, but he could still form recognizable words.

He'd chosen to hide this from Behemoth, but now that cat was out of the bag.

Billy motioned with his head toward the piss bucket, and Behemoth, at last, relented, removing the leather straps so his prisoner

34

could uncork his kidneys and clean up the mess in his jeans as best he could.

When Billy laid down to be re-trussed, he swelled his chest and stiffened and slightly bowed out his arms from his sides. When he sat up, he instantly became aware of the greater play in his ties. He kept his arms flexed against the slack.

Behemoth, still distracted by his own anger, didn't notice.

THAT EVENING, the crazed derelict busied himself with a project that involved wrapping one end of a green branch with rags picked from the pile where he'd hidden the gun. The bough was about two feet long and two inches wide. He made his selections carefully, choosing longer pieces of cotton cloth that were at least a foot wide, pulling them snugly to the wood, then placing birch bark between each layer of cloth.

He looked to be constructing a torch, not unlike the flambeau from Billy's dream about Matt sitting up in the underground coffin.

For his part, Billy was glad to have the attention off him.

He decided he'd initiate his escape attempt after Behemoth fell asleep. Billy only needed to free one hand, feel for the Colt Commander, then bring the firearm up blazing. If the plan failed, he was good as dead, but he figured he was probably good as dead anyway if he did nothing.

That's not to say Billy was suddenly a paragon of courage. Far from it. He had never been so afraid in his whole life. Fear radiated from his stomach clear through to his fingers, the crown of his head, and the tips of his toes. He even felt it in his ears. And he knew when it came time to act, he'd have to fight through all that fear while remaining level-headed enough to raise and aim the pistol, and—for the first time in his life—kill another human being, or at least wound him badly enough to get away.

Carrying all that fear around was exhausting. That, combined with uneasy sleep on the previous night worked against him, his eyes grew gritty, and his lids began to blink. He fought to stay awake. His plan, after all, was to outlast Behemoth, but you know what they say about best-laid plans.

It didn't seem like he'd slept very long, but it was long enough. Long enough for Behemoth to finish his project, climb on top of him, and lift high the now-flaming torch.

"Your spirit is darkened, corrupted and broken!" the madman shouted. "As good vines, if they are neglected, are oppressed with weeds and thorns and at last killed by them, so are the spirits of such a man!"

Then he brought down the fiery brand and jammed it into Billy's right eye socket.

Billy screamed into a whiteness that shot like lightning into his skull. He twisted and bucked under a pain so searing it clawed his thoughts to shreds. He animated every extremity in a desperate effort to shake off the blistering heat, fighting against the leather straps that bound him, finding the slack but flailing inside it.

Unflinching, Behemoth pressed down the torch, erasing all of Billy's awareness of the pain in his mouth. The maniac sizzled the lid from Billy's eye. The skin on his cheek and eyebrow sputtered, grew boils, and cracked open. Billy heard the soft whistle of his eyeball deflating and felt vitreous jelly drip down the side of his head.

Somehow, he managed to fight one arm through the restraints, used it to prop himself up, still screaming—howling to the gods from his crucible of anguish. He felt the weight shift on his chest. Behemoth fell backward, not off of Billy but onto his lower legs. Squinting his remaining eye toward the heap of rags where the pistol lay, Billy skidded to one side, lunging toward the pile and reaching, reaching, even as his torturer scrambled crablike up his frame, still clutching the torch.

Behemoth's arm came down hard, and the fire bit into Billy's good eye, burning its way into his flesh, nearly into his brain.

He twisted and writhed, his hand now slapping amid the rags for the feel of metal. Then, suddenly, its coolness grazed a knuckle and, lurching again, he managed to seize the pistol by the grip. In his swirl of maddening misery, with the business end of the brand scorching into his face, Billy lifted the gun and fired.

Again and again, until the last round left the barrel.

36

The torch rolled from his face, and the madman's bulk fell from Billy's legs to the ground beyond. Billy listened for the sound of breathing at his feet, but his ears still rang from the thunderclaps of the discharging Colt Commander, and he quickly became too immersed in his own suffering to pay any more heed to his captor or his captor's fate.

How long did he lie on his back in the cave? Hours, perhaps days.

He experienced spells of painful clarity in which his face ached to the very bone, in which his shrieks echoed back at him with clamorous intensity, in which he grappled in the dirt and grit for some ledge on which to rest the tattered remnants of his sanity. Then he was suctioned once again from consciousness into a dark whirlpool he shared with paralytic-featured madmen, ghostly friends, and giant, fang-toothed serpents.

Bit by bit, he worked his way out of his restraints. He crawled toward the cool breeze coming from the cave's entrance, groping with his hands. He left his stone prison, rose to his feet, and barked in deep and guttural babblement, "Help! I need help!"

Luck, finally, was with him. He was out only for a few minutes before a rescuer heard his cries. Yes, he had been missed and reported missing by Wash and other friends, by his parents, and his Uncle Buster, who all joined in the search for him.

"Oh, my God," a woman's voice said. He didn't recognize her voice, but he recognized what it represented. "Billy, is that you? Who did this to you?"

Billy began swaying on his feet, unconsciousness again creeping into the blackness that had replaced his sense of sight. He replied weakly, "His name was Behemoth, for he occupied with his breast a waste wilderness in the garden where the elect and the righteous dwell." But between his swoon and his missing tongue, he wasn't sure if his words were clear enough for her to understand.

"Over here! Over here!" the woman shouted to others, who he heard scrambling toward him through the trees and in the grass.

They carried him off, as he wavered in and out of awareness, from the forest where he left his tongue and his sight.

The madman they found dead on the floor of the cave, united perhaps in the afterlife with his horrid deity.

Leftovers

"'Thou art a pitiful remnant, a half-eaten scrap from the table of
Death,,, '"
—Leonid Andreyev, "Lazarus"

She emptied the drawer onto the kitchen table. The contents crashed and clattered. This drawer had belonged to him. It contained his stuff: a pair of pliers, measuring tape, a peanut can full of screws, tubes of adhesives, paper scraps written on in his Cro-Magnon cursive. Man stuff. It even smelled like man stuff. It had that trapped, flat, iron smell that man stuff tends to have.

As she spread the contents on the table, a flesh-colored cylinder about three inches long rolled out. It was a human finger cleanly cut from a hand, calloused on the inner ridges, its nail thick and gray.

Just below the knuckle, a wedding band gleamed.

His wedding band. *His* finger.

She picked it up. Sniffed it. Weighed it in her palm. She wanted to poke it with her tongue but decided that would be unsanitary. She remembered this finger tracing her shoulder, her ribs, the downy silkiness of her thighs where they vanished beneath her skirt.

She had once been in love with the owner of this finger. Still was, if she was being honest. Not that it mattered anymore, feelings being powerless in a material world.

She swept the finger and the other contents of the drawer off the table and into a black plastic trash bin, where they landed with a roar that emptied her lungs and triggered a twinge that made her feel as if her heart had become dented, not by the man stuff but by all the memories the man stuff stirred up. Wobbly chair legs fixed, spice rack hung, doorbell installed. Like falling dominoes, one remembrance tipped into another.

She stared into the folds of the kitchen curtains as if mesmerized by the design, her mind a million miles off. When this particular movie reel had emptied, she stood and fitted the drawer back onto its mounting brackets and slid it flush.

It would be nice to have an extra kitchen drawer to use.

NOW, MOST NIGHTS, she slept on the couch instead of in her bed, falling asleep either reading a book or watching a movie. It didn't matter which book or which movie. Her concentration was spotty, and she couldn't remember much of what she'd seen or read anyway. Her sleep was fleeting, an hour or two at a time. She was up and down all night, riding the rails of anxiety and depression.

Her doctor had prescribed fluoxetine for her nerves, but it took a while to build up in her system. Hence, the only effect she felt immediately was occasional dizziness. She could have gotten something to help her sleep, but she didn't want to overdo it on the meds.

Not like her mother had.

One day, Mom had shown all the pills in the medicine cabinet to her and explained what they were for: hydrocodone for arthritis, simvastatin for cholesterol, lisinopril for high blood pressure, levothyroxine for a thyroid condition, amlodipine besylate for blood flow, omeprazole for acid reflux, azithromycin for sinusitis, metformin for borderline diabetes. There must have been twenty different types of drugs. Her mom had explained that some were for before meals, some after, some in the morning, some at noon, and some at bedtime.

"Mom, are you sure you need all these medicines?"

Mom had shrugged. "When you get to be my age, you take what the doctor gives you. You don't question. For all I know, these pills are all that's keeping me alive."

Mom was eighty-six at the time. She never made it to eighty-seven.

That's when he chose to leave her, when her mother died. He'd said they'd grown apart but was it really that bad? There was no adultery, as far as she knew. There were no arguments about money, workloads, or intimacy. Neither of them had wanted children. When they disagreed, they largely agreed to disagree. Amiably, even. Like adults do.

"There are no highs or lows with us," he'd said. "We just sort of putter along on a flat plane that goes nowhere."

In the garage was his work table. He'd taken the tools with him and all that was left of them were outlines on a pegboard. There were boxes of books stacked against the back wall: some hers, some his. She didn't have the energy to sort out whose were whose. She doubted she ever would. The spot where he'd parked his car remained noticeably vacant, deliberately unused. She still parked to the far left, as she'd always done, leaving room for his vehicle—for his *phantom* auto. So why was she still careful to allow plenty of room for it? Habit? Wishful thinking?

He'd come to her mother's funeral with her. She gave him credit for that. It was the last time they went anywhere together.

The divorce papers came in the mail. She thought of calling him and asking, "Isn't there still a chance for us?" But she didn't. She'd signed the papers in the presence of her friend Darlene, a notary. Darlene stamped the papers with her notary stamp and added her signature.

Once the papers were in the mail drop at Cub Foods, it was all over.

After that, she'd walked around the store like she was any other shopper on any other day. She filled her cart with apples and pears that would wither away uneaten in her fruit bowl, with bread that would go moldy and soy milk that would turn, and dairy-free ice cream destined to grow freezer burns. She'd eat some of the food. She had to eat some of it.

When she went to grab the grocery bags from her trunk, she noticed a leg lying on the trunk's ochre carpeting, a human leg, from the ankle to the knee. His leg, of course. He always had muscular calves, though his thighs had gone a little flabby. That's alright. It's part of growing old. So, she never said a word about it.

She brushed her fingertips across the little hairs that covered the leg from the ankle to the knee. Funny, the things you come to miss.

41

She recalled their vacation in Florida, that time they went to the ocean, with its smooth, damp shore and languidly churning waters. Her on the spread blanket, him walking barefoot at the rim of the ocean's foamy reach. Him in baggy cargo shorts, shirtless, the sun dancing on the golden hairs of his legs.

How old were they then? Was it that long ago?

In her memories, they were always ageless, and everything happened about three years ago. That was her standard answer when asked how long ago something had happened: "I don't know. Maybe three years ago."

He'd laugh at this and say, "No—more like five. We went there on our anniversary. Remember?"

She'd come to rely on him for orientation in her life: for when it was that they had taken that cruise to the Bahamas; for simple directions like north and south when they drove around town; for how they were related to relatives ("He's your second cousin on your father's side."); for when was the last time they'd mowed the front lawn; or for the name of that restaurant in Bloomington that had the spicy falafels she so loved; or the name of that neighbor down the street who they only saw once a year on National Night Out.

By having a husband, she'd always known where she was, where she was going and how all things related to her and him.

She was going to carry the leg to the garbage can but instead decided to leave it.

Closing the trunk, she toted her bags to the front door and set them on the stoop while she fished keys from her purse.

The next time she opened her trunk, the leg was gone. Oh, well. She was sure it would eventually turn up one day. Somewhere.

WHEN SHE WAS A LITTLE GIRL, her mother told her that spiders would crawl into her throat if she slept with her mouth open.

"The average person swallows eight spiders a year in their sleep," Mom said. "It's true."

Of course, it wasn't true at all, but as a little girl, she'd believed it. Back then, she believed everything her mom said.

Back then, she would sometimes fall asleep wondering what type of spider might crawl down her throat that night. She knew there was a fuzzy, black one in the basement that she called Charlotte, but that one never seemed to wander very far from her web. Still, there was a gossamer egg sack hanging in the spider's den, and baby spiders would scamper off and could easily fit down a person's throat.

One day, she'd spotted a daddy long leg hiding in a dark corner of the living room. She remembered wondering how the spider could fit down her throat with those long legs. Maybe the legs could be folded somehow. They seemed to be hinged.

Now, an older version of that child on all fours in her bedroom was remembering about her mother and the spiders.

A common house spider was creeping across her bedroom carpet, and she uneasily held a wine goblet in one hand that she would use to trap it. The spider, about three-quarters of an inch long, had a dull, coffee-bean body and legs that were a medley of golds and browns. She'd seen this kind of spider all her life, but she'd never attempted to catch one before. That task had always fallen to someone else.

He sometimes trapped the spiders to appease her, but generally smashed them with a shoe. He wielded the shoe like a hammer, striking three times (*whump-whump-whump*). She had to look away when he did this. Once she'd caught a glimpse of a spider leg twitching from among gooey, massacred leavings. She imagined the tiny creature was waving goodbye to this world, having been crushed by an overwhelming and unmerciful foe.

Yet, to him, the spider's life was meaningless. His for the taking.

She brought down the goblet, and the spider realized at once something was up. It froze, flexed, then began a tentative crawl around the inside of the cup's perimeter. The tricky part would be sliding cardboard under the glass in such a way as to keep from damaging the spider's legs. Having accomplished this, she carried her arachnid prisoner downstairs and into the backyard for release.

As the tiny creature scurried away, she felt good. For an instant.

HER GIRLFRIEND, Darlene Grimwood, called her later that week to see how she was doing.

"Okay, I guess," she said. "After being married for almost twenty-five years, it's an adjustment."

"You'll be fine. Remember: a woman without a man is like a fish without a bicycle." Darlene, a proud, fifty-something single, chuckled on the phone line. "Don't let it get to you, my friend."

"Easier said than done."

"Tell you what. Let's have lunch. Snap you out of your blues. How does Panera's in Maple Grove sound? Or we could go to that Noodles place you like."

"Thanks, Darlene, but I don't have much of an appetite these days." She eyed the man's foot on her kitchen table, veined in faint blue, callused, and orange at the heel. He always had the ugliest toes.

"You have to eat, dear. Tell you what: we'll go to Noodles. My treat. Tomorrow at noon. Whaddya say?"

"Alright." She pinched the foot, watched it redden.

"Is there anything else I can do?"

She was silent for a moment. Then, she said, "It's just ... He's everywhere, Darlene. He's in my dreams, he's in my thoughts. How can it be so easy for him to walk away, and so hard for me? To him, it's a new beginning. To me, it just feels like the end ... of everything."

The next day, her phone rang.

Darlene. "I'm at Noodles. Where are you? Are you coming?"

"Sorry, Darlene. I'm not feeling very well. Might be catching a cold."

"Do you want me to bring you something back? Japanese pan noodles? Tomato bisque?"

"No, I just need to rest. Thanks anyway. Sorry to let you down."

That afternoon, she walked from room to room in her pajamas, in a daze.

LATER THAT MONTH, she took all the photos from the walls and shelves. Not just the ones he was in, but all of them. She didn't want them around reminding her of the life they'd once shared. She put these in grocery bags and carried them up to the attic.

She emptied from the refrigerator that gawdawful horseradish mustard he favored; the pickled dragon fruit he brought home on a whim from the Asian market in Brooklyn Park but never opened; half a carton of ... *the hell with it.* She cleared out everything, and dumped it all in the trash. Every jar, every bottle, every package, every Tupperware bowl. She did the same thing with the freezer compartment. Then she pulled from the naked ice box the crispers, the glass ledge, the trays and the door guards: every removable part, she removed and stacked in the sink.

She scrubbed the white plastic interior of the fridge till it was shiny and new-looking. She filled the sink with soapy water and scoured off years' worth of drippings and smudges and spills till every trace was gone. Till every trace of *him* was gone.

In the course of her daily routines, she sometimes came upon a sock of his or a T-shirt or some other item that was either his or reminded her of him. These she threw away, but not before sniffing them first. Breathing in their aromas one last time.

The autumn passed, long and lethargic. Sometimes she felt like her old self. Sometimes she had no clue who she was.

The next time she made a lunch date with Darlene, she showed. She ate a small salad and had a drink from the pop machine. Darlene did most of the talking, but she contributed as well. It felt good to be out in public doing something that people do out in public, her voice blending in with the general drone of conversation.

Afterward, they walked around the pond in Town Green park.

"We should do this more often," Darlene said.

"Yes. I'd like that."

Winter came as it usually does in Minnesota. One minute the backyard was overcast and full of dead leaves. The next minute, snow swept in, covering everything. And you just knew that the cold spell that came with the flurries was the beginning of what would seem like forever.

One morning when she sat on the couch, eating cereal and watching TV, one of the newscasters, a young blonde woman with a Polish name, talked of how slippery roads had caused a fatal accident on Highway 100 in Robbinsdale. Three people were killed. Two of the names were people she'd never heard of.

But one she most definitely had.

45

She turned, misty-eyed, to the severed head on the couch next to her and said, "You always were slow to adapt to winter driving."

Father Christmas Don't Come Around Here No More

"'Ho! Ho!' laughed Gabriel Grub, as he sat himself down on a flat tombstone which was a favourite resting-place of his; and drew forth his wicker bottle. 'A coffin at Christmas! A Christmas Box. Ho! ho! ho!'"
— Charles Dickens, "The Goblins Who Stole a Sexton"

From the start, Lydia Bassett could see it was a bad fit. The would-be parents, in their sixties, were too old to handle such a troubled child, and their thick, Austrian accents made communicating with the boy difficult.

"What did she say?" Bobby Gore asked, scrunching his nose.

Bobby had just turned eight and had already been ejected from two foster homes. Lydia feared he was already working on banishment from a third.

She gave him a cross look that he pretended not to notice. "Mrs. Krenn asked what your favorite TV shows are." She puckered her lips.

He squinted into Sabine Krenn's long, lined face as if she'd just asked him the dumbest question in the world. "I don't know. I like shows with killers in them."

"*Kee*-lahs?" The tall, thin woman wore a puzzled expression. "You mean like cowboys ahnd Indians? Shoot 'em ups?"

Bobby shook his head. "You know, like knifers and things. Serial killers."

Bobby grinned, and Lydia caught a look in the boy's eyes that chilled her blood.

"Bobby's pretty good at baseball, coloring, and card games," Lydia said, trying not to sound distracted.

"I slay at Crazy Eights," he said.

Gus Krenn stood behind his wife, eyeing the boy, saying nothing. Gus did repairs at a sewing center in Plymouth, and Sabine volunteered at a nursing home in St. Louis Park. They'd never had any children of their own, but as they neared retirement age, Sabine felt the longing to be motherly, or maybe grandmotherly, and to have someone with whom to share their home, their twilight years, and the modest inheritance that allowed them to live life according to their simple needs. They'd been on the list of potential adoptive parents for more than three years and normally would still be waiting.

But Bobby Gore was a special case.

Bobby lost his mother and father to a violent episode two years ago. He said later he couldn't remember what their argument had been about (he was, after all, only six at the time), but he recalled his parents were always bickering about something. One night, his mother, an English professor at Bemidji State University given to fits of melancholy, had simply lost it, and beaten her husband to death with one of Bobby's baseball bats: a 32-inch, maplewood Louisville Slugger the boy had received for his birthday. Before Bobby's horrified eyes, she'd repeatedly beat the father's head until the skull cracked open like a Cadbury Creme Easter Egg. Then, she fetched a long-barreled scattergun from a closet shelf, opened her mouth to it, and pulled the trigger.

The noise of the shotgun blast alerted the neighbors, who called the police. When they arrived on the scene, the cops found Bobby watching Sponge Bob SquarePants on the TV in the living room while his all-but-headless parents lay in carnage on the kitchen floor.

The cops said the boy had a blank look in his eyes and was generally unresponsive.

Children of the Lamb, the adoption agency Lydia worked for, smoothed over Bobby's background. All the agency revealed to prospective adopters was that Bobby's parents had died in a gun mishap, the graphic nature of the event judged unnecessarily gruesome and off-putting.

"Do you zink you would like living heah?" Sabine asked him.

"Zink?" He scrunched his nose again.

"Bobby." It was all Lydia could do to keep from losing her temper. "You understand what she means. Answer her."

Bobby looked around the small living room with its bookshelves, antique furniture, and corner phonograph with stacked vinyl albums. He studied Sabine and Gus for a moment, then shrugged. "Can I get a PlayStation?"

Sabine's face lit up. "Ziss very day we will tahke you to Tahget ahnd get you ze very best PlayStahtion zey hahve."

"And games?"

"Ahnd gahmes."

"Mmmmm. Alright."

"Okay, zen. It's a deal."

Sabine seemed elated. Gus looked not so sure.

He scratched at his disappearing hairline and frowned at the boy.

FATHER CHRISTMAS. That's what the Krenns called Santa Claus. Must be an Austrian thing. Who cares anyway? Santa Claus, Father Christmas, the Easter Bunny: it was all one big lie. A joke on the kids who were dumb enough to believe in that stuff.

Bobby had read in a book once that Santa was based on the Norse god Odin, who flew over houses on an eight-legged horse, dropping loaves of bread to children. Bread. For Christmas. Big deal. And an eight-legged horse? Kids back then must have been dumber than rocks.

But Bobby had to admit, that first year with the Krenns, Father Christmas was awfully generous.

Besides a profusion of new video games, he received a fielder's mitt, ball and bat; a remote-controlled race car; a basketball; a scooter; a science set with a robotic arm; a spin and spiral art station; a Lego model car kit; and collector tins of Pokémon cards.

Sabine—was he supposed to call her Mom now?—had wrapped the presents in colorful paper, even putting a ribbon and bow on each one, which Bobby had never even heard of before. She'd stacked them neatly under a REAL tree bought at Harbo's Garden Center. Bobby had helped the Krenns pick it out, which was alright since they stopped afterward at Dairy Queen.

Overall, it was a much better Christmas than he'd ever had before—in terms of his haul, anyway. Christmas dinner was alright, though a little heavier on the vegetables than Bobby would've preferred. He cleaned his plate anyway. It was the least he could do to make Sabine happy.

Gus, he was a different animal altogether. Bobby thought of him as the Gray Man, on account of his hair (what little he had left) and his moustache being ashen gray, and he always seemed to wear a fine coat of gray dust over his clothes and the rest of him. Or maybe that was just Bobby's imagination.

The only time the Gray Man ever smiled was when Sabine got excited about something. Even then, though, it was sort of a sourpuss grin. He hardly ever spoke to Bobby, mostly just looked at him like the boy had three heads or something.

Even on Christmas day, about all he said to him was, "Mehry Christmahs, Bobby. I hope you like yoah toys."

THE FIRST FAMILY BOBBY had stayed with was the Reillys in Brainerd. This was just after good ol' Mom had brained Dad and swallowed the business end of a Remington double-barreled shotgun. Truth be told, Bobby knew he was a little out of it back then. He kept imagining Mom pounding the pudding out of Dad's noodle. Or Mom spraying her brains like spaghetti sauce all over the kitchen ceiling. These were the little movies that ran in his head, and would start and stop with no warning. He still saw them sometimes, but mostly they just played in his dreams.

He was talking to a shrink back then, an old coot name Dr. Linkman, who wore a white doctor's coat and always had a pack of Lucky Strikes in his breast pocket.

Peter Reilly—that was the father's name—would drop him off and pick him up at Dr. Linkman's office every Monday evening for an hour of consultation.

Peter was a fat, easygoing man with a bushy black beard who worked as an engineer for Burlington Northern Railroad, which was a pretty good job to have in Brainerd. He drove a Ford F-150 Raptor and always played CDs of polka music in the cab. At home, Peter liked to watch professional wrestling and drink Pig's Eye beer.

His wife, Jocelyn, not exactly a stunner, worked as a cashier at the Tom Thumb grocery store. Her feet would get swollen from being on them all day and, after work, she soaked them, all bloated and veiny, in a tub with Epsom salt to get some kind of relief.

They had a daughter named Arlet. Her hair was thin and stringy, and she was small for her age, but otherwise, she was alright. A year older than Bobby, she was always soft-spoken and polite, even though kids at school teased her something terrible, calling her Arlet the Leprechaun, because of her size.

For Christmas, the Reillys bought him mostly clothes. He did get a pretty cool belt buckle with a longhorn steer on it, but otherwise, it was your standard jeans and flannel shirts, a new robe, slippers, and, as an afterthought, a box of checkers.

Checkers. Like anybody played checkers anymore.

It was never clear to him whether the Reillys ever planned to adopt him or just rake in the government checks for fostering him. Jocelyn always patted him on the head when she came home from work, gave Arlet a hug, and asked the two of them how their day went. This resulted in about five minutes' worth of conversation, then she headed straight for her tub and her Epsom salt, and planted herself on the couch to watch TV. It was pointless trying to talk with her the rest of the evening, her being so totally tuned in to the shows. About the only thing she ever responded to was a suggestion—made during a commercial—that they whip up a bowl of popcorn in the air popper, which Arlet *only* was trusted to operate. That was about the extent of his interaction with Jocelyn.

Peter ran hot and cold. If he was in a good mood, like during a WWE match on a Saturday afternoon, he could be congenial as a beauty-contest winner, joking with the kids and maybe slipping them a buck or two to go buy candy at GasBuddy. Other times, he'd get hush and walk around the house acting as if his best friend had just died.

51

Sometimes when he drove Bobby to see Dr. Linkman, Peter would jack his polka tunes way high and just stare in silence at the traffic like he was headed for a beatdown from Mike Tyson.

Dinners at the Reillys' consisted mainly of canned foods: ravioli, stews, veggies (usually corn), Spam, Hormel chili, soups, anything you could crack open with a can opener and heat in three minutes in a microwave. Billy actually enjoyed this aspect of living there since all of his favorite foods were canned.

But he had to admit the best thing about living with the Reillys was Arlet, scrawny little Arlet. Besides being sweet and polite and sharing, she always was up for doing things Bobby liked, even if she was no good at them. They talked for hours, and he even told her things that he never told anyone but Dr. Linkman. Dark stuff. Things like how his mother sometimes chased him with a shotgun through his dreams with her head blown off.

And there was something else about Arlet: she awoke in him the first tinglings of not necessarily desire but of genuine curiosity about girls. About how they had something completely different from what he did going on under their clothes.

The two of them were studying these differences when Peter caught them one night.

The next day, Jocelyn packed Bobby's things, and a blue-and-gold van from Children of the Lamb arrived to haul him away. He never saw the Reillys again. Never saw Dr. Linkman. Never saw Arlet.

His fake family was gone, like it never existed.

Funny, it was there a minute ago.

He'd been halfway through first grade at the time, and had to switch from a rural school to an urban one midstream. Not that Groveland Elementary was a tough school by St. Paul standards. Still, in Brainerd, the kids had never bothered him much. In St. Paul, he learned to fight if he wanted to keep his lunch money.

As it turned out, Bobby had a knack for fighting. Pretty soon, he was taking other kids' lunch money.

He stayed at the time with Charlie and Alena Wu, a middle-aged Chinese-American couple; their son, Ezra, who was nine then; and one other foster kid, an eleven-year-old white boy named Gerald Bronski, who everyone called Mookie. They were all nice to Bobby. He had his own bedroom with a TV in it, and there weren't too many rules—just pick up after yourself, that kind of thing.

Charlie worked at the Minnesota Historical Society on Kellogg Boulevard as a software developer. Arlena worked part-time at Trader Joe's on Lexington Parkway. They both wore rimless, oval eyeglasses, and whenever Bobby approached them with a question or an announcement, they gave him their wholly undivided attention. He got the feeling they weren't fostering kids just for the money. They got something more out of it.

The first few months, things were fairly copasetic. He palled around with Ezra and, to a lesser extent, Mookie. They'd skateboard around the neighborhood, play baseball with local kids, go to the movies, and occasionally swipe candy or Matchbox toy cars from stores on Grand Avenue. He settled comfortably into this new lifestyle. He could even see himself maybe living with the Wus forever.

Oh, sure, Charlie and Alena were called into the principal's office a few times over Bobby's bullying of the other students. At one meeting, they were even presented with a doctor's bill for stitches. The principal also told them that Bobby enjoyed being disruptive in classes and often talked back to teachers. He'd called the school's mental-health counselor a B-I-T-C-H. Alena flushed at this bit of news

"Bobby, you have to behave yourself at school or they're going to kick you out," Charlie had warned.

But that was about all the Wus could muster, as far as disciplining him was concerned, and the prospect of being tossed from Groveland Elementary didn't exactly have him shaking in his boots.

Then, one Saturday night after Charlie and Alena had gone to bed, he and Mookie had snuck out with a BB-gun pistol Mookie had borrowed from a friend, and shot up some neighborhood windows. They were having a good time, taking turns shooting, laughing it up uncontrollably every time glass shattered, getting lightheaded from all the running around and laughing.

Until the police showed up.

Mookie got clean away, scrambling back to the Wu house before anyone else even knew he was gone. Bobby was not as lucky. He got nabbed by the Man in a back alley, caught red-handed with the BB-gun, and hauled to the cop shop from which his foster parents were called to collect him.

The Wus ended up paying five-thousand dollars for broken windows and got the neighbors to drop charges against Bobby on the understanding the boy would permanently leave their community.

A familiar blue-and-gold van showed up at the Wus the next day to cart Bobby off to his new home.

UNLIKE THE REILLYS AND THE WUS, the Krenns never gave up on Bobby. Okay, to be fair, Sabine Krenn never gave up on him. Gus Krenn, the Gray Man, was never really onboard in the first place. But Gus went along with everything, including the adoption, because he could see it pleased his wife to no end.

On Bobby's ninth birthday, they threw a party, inviting all the kids in his third-grade class for cake and ice cream, and party games at their house on Winnetka Avenue in New Hope. Only two of the kids who were invited came—a runny-nosed little goblin named Hector, who'd been over before playing Tomb Raider with Bobby, and a burr-haired Latina named Constance, who Bobby didn't even know was in his class.

If the scant turnout bothered Sabine, she wasn't letting on. She merrily dished up birthday cake, refereed pin the tail on the donkey, and handed out prizes as if it were the happiest day of her life. The Gray Man wanted to skip the party, but Sabine insisted he stay, which he did, watching the proceedings glumly from his La-Z-Boy recliner.

By the time Bobby was in fourth grade, he was already earning a reputation at Meadow Lake Elementary School for being a troublemaker, and with the New Hope Police Department for shoplifting, vandalism, and truancy.

"Mr. and Mrs. Krenn, this boy needs counseling," a patrolwoman who escorted Bobby home in a squad car told them.

"He's just going trew a phahse, is ahll," Sabine replied. "Boys will be boys."

"If he doesn't get straightened out soon, you're going to wind up one of these days visiting him in prison."

The Grey Man raised an eyebrow and cast Bobby a steely glare.

They brought him to a child psychologist in Plymouth, a Dr. Viggo Beltman, a recent graduate of the University of Minnesota. Dr. Viggo, fresh-faced and pleasant, had a knack for talking to kids, and Bobby took to him at once, not because the good doctor was wise and understanding of kids' problems, but because Bobby soon figured out he could tell this guy anything, and he'd believe him. It became a game.

Dr. Viggo would say things like, "Why do you think you're having such a hard time in school?"

Bobby would reply, "It's like I speak a different language than these city kids. They don't understand me, and I don't understand them. And they're mean. I once had a kid push me up against the hall lockers and walloped me so hard my lower teeth almost punched through my lip."

Which was basically true, except Bobby had been the one throwing the punch.

"I see," Dr. Viggo would say, and he'd go all down in the mouth.

Or the doctor would ask, "How are things going at home?"

And Bobby would say something like, "The food isn't very good. But they're from Austria, and it's probably considered pretty good food in Austria. Lots of green beans." Or: "He doesn't say much and she never stops talking. And they always take sides against me, with the teachers and the cops. It's like the whole world is against me. Can't they see that I'm the real victim here?"

And so on.

Dr. Viggo told the Krenns Bobby was making great progress. The sad part of it was: the psychologist believed it.

After a while, even Sabine began to doubt the visits were working. But this was toward the end.

Every Sunday, the Krenns dressed him up in a suit—a monkey suit, Bobby liked to call it—and took him to St. Alfonzo Catholic Church, where they could show him off. Sabine was usually quite cheerful on these excursions, but one Sunday she seemed less so. And the next Sunday, even less so. When the third Sunday came around, they stayed home from church, and Sabine spent the day in bed.

The week before Thanksgiving, he and Hector were returning from school when they discovered Bobby's house in a stir. Uniformed EMTs were wheeling a gurney out the front door and through the snow to a waiting ambulance. On the gurney, unconscious and colorless, lay Sabine, an oxygen mask on her face.

"Huhry, Bobby," Gus said. "We hahve to go to ze hospitahl."

By the time they got to North Memorial Hospital in Robbinsdale, it was all over. Sabine was gone. Her heart had given out, the emergency-room doctor informed them. There was nothing more they could do.

When Bobby looked from the doctor to Gus Krenn, he saw the Gray Man looking back at him with murderous intent.

BAD MITTERNDORF WAS AN ALPINE VILLAGE of about five-thousand in west-central Austria. It's where two championship ski jumpers and the winner of the 2014 Eurovision Song Contest lived. The place was known for its health resorts, thermal baths, canoeing on the Salza-Stausee reservoir, and wildlife areas, hiking trails, parks, and restaurants. And it's just sixty miles from Salzburg, where *The Sound of Music* was filmed.

Bad Mitterndorf also happened to be the birthplace of Gus and Sabine Krenn. The two grew up just across Mitterrndorferstrasse from one another and were friends as far back as either of them could recall, Sabine had told Bobby many times. "Gustahv was ahlways ze only mahn foah me," she would say.

On the train from Graz Airport, Gus said very little, preferring to stare out the window at the snow-covered countryside, no doubt reminiscing. Bobby did nothing to break the Gray Man's reverie. These days he was especially careful not to bother his adoptive father. He and Gus had never gotten along that well when Sabine was alive. Now, they had almost nothing to say to one another. In fact, Bobby had only learned of their impending trip to Austria two days before they departed.

"We ahh going to spend Christmahs wiss my fahmily ziss yeeuh," the Gray Man had said. "Wiss my mothah ahnd brothah ahnd uncles."

The train ride from Graz Airport took about two hours. The batteries had run out on Bobby's Nintendo 3DS portable gaming device somewhere over the North Atlantic Ocean and, of course, Gus had neglected to pack spares. On the plane, Bobby had watched an in-flight movie, the 2015 remake of *Poltergeist*, which was nowhere near as scary as the original, but it helped pass the time. The train, however, offered no movies or alternatives to its passengers and, other than, say, reading a book (a comical suggestion in Bobby's case), there was nothing to divert his attention from the tedious journey. He was reduced to watching other riders, staring at the passing scenery, and daydreaming.

He thought about Sabine, who he'd never really thought about much when she was alive. He considered how her passing had affected him personally, and he resented it. Resented the absence of her doting on him, placating him, giving in to nearly his every wish. Resented the vacuum her death had left in his life—a vacuum Gus Krenn appeared loathe to fill.

At Sabine's wake, Bobby had overheard Gus say to a coworker from the sewing center, "Ze boy woah hah down. Whahtevah ze doctahs say, I will go to my grahve believing Bobby killed hah."

Killed her? But he was just a kid, getting into the sort of trouble kids get into all the time. And if he took advantage of her kindness, well, she was a soft touch whenever he flashed his "poor-orphan" eyes. Who could blame him?

The Gray Man blamed him; that was who.

Now Bobby felt adrift with a nemesis in a foreign land, where people spoke another language and had unfamiliar customs, and the houses didn't look like American houses, and almost every driver drove a high-end car—a BMW or a Porsche—though most Austrians, it seemed, just walked everywhere, usually accompanied by their dogs. Stores closed early, and beer drinking was rampant. Such a weird place.

What if Gus just walks away and leaves me here somewhere in a crowd? He could imagine the Gray Man doing that. *How would I get back home?*

Like it or not, he would have to *try* to behave, at least until he was back in the good old U.S.A.

The Krenn residence on Mitterrndorferstrasse reminded Bobby of a gingerbread house, a two-story version of one, painted in pastry colors—brownie brown and icing pink—and it had the narrow frame

Bobby associated with gingerbread houses. There were no Christmas lawn decorations, but the windows were lit up with colorful lights.

Gus Krenn's mother, Anja, a stooped matronly, age-spotted version of the Gray Man, shuffled to the door to greet them. Anja hugged her son and they spoke excitedly in German for several minutes. When it came to Bobby, the boy's reputation must have proceeded him because when, at last, Anja turned her attention to the boy, the old woman frowned at him and studied him as if he were a lizard in a terrarium. It was with a great show of reluctance that Anja reached out and ruffled Bobby's hair. She nodded to the boy but did not smile.

A brief entryway led to the living room, which was maybe three-quarters the size of an average American living room. Bobby removed his jacket and sat on a two-cushion loveseat in front of the television, which was tuned to a news program. While Gus and Anja jibber-jabbered in German, Bobby took in the room: the wooden knickknack cabinets with their sheets of beveled glass; the framed pictures of smiling Austrian faces; the recliner where he imagined Anja spent most of her time; antique end tables; overfilled bookshelves; a cozy place for a geezer a half-step from death's doorway.

Here and there were Christmas decorations, mostly religious: a creche, tin angels, candles with crosses on them, a collector's plate of the three wise men journeying across a starlit desert. There was one Santa-like figurine, Father Christmas, dressed more like the pope than jolly old St. Nick, but he had the long, white beard and a sack of presents on his back. Two other figurines stood next to him. One was a fur-covered man-creature with horns that curled back on his head; the other an insane-looking old woman standing on one leg and clutching a huge knife. These latter two could have stepped out of a Clive Barker movie.

Bobby rose to his feet and approached the statuettes, which were displayed in one of the knickknack cabinets.

There was something awful about these figures, something beyond just being frightful in appearance. Bobby sensed they were, for lack of a better word, evil. Just plain evil. Evilness radiated from them like static electricity.

The furry man with the horns had a gawdawful grimace, his eyes shining with bad intent, his mouth a fang-lined cavern. His clawed hands curled out as if about to clutch at Bobby. The old woman—a wild-eyed, demonic, beak-nosed crone—appeared to be dancing with joy at the prospect of wielding her blade.

Bobby shuddered.

When he turned to ask about the figures, both Gus and Anja were peering at him silently, as if in possession of a shared dark secret.

"Wh-who are these people next to Santa?" he asked.

Gus and Anja exchanged a look, then Gus replied, "Zey ahh Krahmpus ahnd Frau Pehchta. Zey come aht Christmahstime foah ze bahd boys ahnd guhls."

Bobby scrunched his nose and turned back to the showcase. He wouldn't want either one of those two coming for him. Even Father Christmas seemed to be wearing a scowl.

Dinner that night was some sort of cabbage soup served with fibrous crackers that were almost too hard to chew. These Gus devoured as if they were a Pizza Lucé gourmet pizza with double toppings and a side order of chicken nuggets. Content to ignore him, Gus and Anja kept up their German banter, accompanied by laughter and tears and winsome expressions. They went on this way, throughout the evening.

At least Anja had hunted up batteries for his Nintendo. He played Splinter Cell until bedtime, glancing occasionally at the sinister Christmas figurines.

The next day Gus' brother, Oskar, an elementary teacher at Hauptschule Bad Mitterndorf, joined them for a breakfast of battered apple rings, which Bobby enjoyed much more than he had last night's soup.

Oskar Krenn, in a collarless wool jacket and blue jeans, was a bald and lightly bearded forty-something with bright blue eyes and a casual manner. He spoke English with virtually no accent and, of the three adults, took the most interest in Bobby.

"How was your flight over, Bobby?" he asked.

"It was okay."

"What do you think of Austria so far?"

"Well, from what I've seen, it's a lot different than America."

Oskar chuckled. "New places will seem different at first, but I think you'll find people everywhere are about the same, good and bad. Do you know what day it is here?"

"Saturday."

"Yes, very good. It's Saturday, December 5. In Bad Mitterndorf, tonight we have a parade that is part of our Christmas festivities. Tonight, we celebrate Krampus. Do you know who Krampus is?"

Bobby remembered the figurine. "Kind of."

"Oh! Krampus is a wicked creature who comes after children who misbehave. Bad children. He's half goat and half demon. His name comes from the German word *Krampen*, which means claw. And he has claws. Claws and fangs. He likes to beat bad children with a whip or birch rods, then carry them off in a big sack to the underworld."

"So, he's bad Santa?"

Oskar laughed again. "Yes, you could call him bad Santa. Very bad Santa. He is, of course, just a myth, but a very ancient one. And you know what they say about ancient myths? There's always a little truth to them."

Bobby wanted to hear more about this Krampus character, but Oskar turned his attention to Gus and Anja, and joined them in speaking German.

Bobby's questions would have to wait until that night's parade.

SECTIONS OF METAL FENCING lined the street for crowd control, and police wearing reflective outer suits mingled with the gathering spectators, sharing good-natured banter while keeping an eye out for troublemakers. Bobby, Gus and Oskar had arrived just as twilight faded to night. A light snow fell on them. It was cold, but not as cold as most December nights in Minnesota.

Bobby leaned against the fencing and looked down the street at a distant ruckus. A policewoman led off an unruly drunken man. The drunk flailed and shouted, while the policewoman, a thickset, no-nonsense type in orange coveralls, guided him off by the collar. Some in the crowd laughed at this but not Bobby. If anything, it made the boy aware of a potentially dangerous element among those surrounding him.

Beyond where the drunken man had been escorted away, three figures came into view. Long reeds of straw draped their bodies, and they wore wooden masks with tall horns that reminded Bobby of insect antennae. They banged the road with brooms of wheat stalks.

"Those are the straw scrapers," Uncle Oskar said. "They're clearing the way for the others."

"Others?"

"You'll see." Oskar's voice hinted at something ominous.

As the straw scrapers grew closer, Bobby felt a sickness begin to rise in him.

The figures wore costumes designed to frighten. Their masks bore monstrous personifications of wickedness—deathly white and grimacing horribly. Their towering horns appeared otherworldly. Besides beating the street, they shook their brooms threateningly at bystanders.

Bobby had thought this celebration would be akin to Halloween festivities in his home country. He'd been to the Minnesota town of Anoka (the self-proclaimed "Halloween Capital of the World") with his friend Hector and with Hector's family, and viewed that city's annual Halloween parade, which featured hundreds of costumed ghouls and fiends. They were a little scary, but not like this. Here, he could feel a frightful tension cranking up in the crowd with each passing minute.

The straw scrapers promenaded by, and Bobby felt relief when they chose others than him to harass.

Next came a trio dressed similar to the altar boys at St. Alfonzo's, collecting money from the crowd. They may have dressed like altar boys, but they were men; tall, skeletal men, their gaunt faces done up in pale-blue makeup. One of them reached out a hand toward Bobby, who handed over a gold-rimmed one-euro coin that Gus had given him. When the server took the coin from Bobby, a spooky feeling passed between them, and the man's demeanor grew suddenly grimmer.

"You hahve not been a good boy ziss yeeuh, hahve you, Bobby?"

"How do you know my name?" the boy demanded.

But the money collector moved past him to beggar coins from others in the crowd, and a stunned Bobby was left to wonder.

He became aware of a general change in the atmosphere—a thickening of the night, a greater harshness of sound, occasional drifts of putrid stench infusing the cool night breeze. His skin pimpled and bunched from a coldness beyond winter's reach.

He could hear Gus and Oskar still yakking behind him, but their voices blended with the noise of the crowd, and he paid them no mind as, before his eyes, a throng of truly horrible characters joined the parade from behind the altar men, swelling the pageant to a throbbing mass of hideous deformity. He felt himself drawn deeper into the fright and gloom these apparitions brought with them.

A humpbacked troll riding a horse mannequin wheeled past, shaking his fist and shouting to the heavens. Death angels with black wings and stark-white faces hoisted impaled skulls. A ghostly night watchman rattled a medieval pole weapon and an ethereally glowing lantern. Behind the watchman, a troop of soot-faced scroll carriers barked out proclamations that Bobby couldn't understand but feared nonetheless.

It was as if the crazies had seized control: the misshapen, the freakish, the savage. Lunatics reveling in their own madness, cavalcading like mindless jokers unleashed from the bowels of the netherworld. The forces of chaos, in full display.

And all Bobby could do was watch.

Spectral devils in death masks danced with their scythes. A blacksmith in a dusky sheepskin coat and dangling iron shackles hammered on the ground near spectators' toes, sparking panicky backward leaps.

Amid all this madness, Father Christmas, in a mitered hat and a floor-length cape, looked over the crowd with hollow eyes. He clutched a gold scepter in one hand and an oversized book (Bobby guessed it was meant to be a Bible) in the other. *Was that blood on the scepter or some trick of the light?*

And these phantasms, Bobby knew with tumultuous certainty, were just warm-ups for the true star of the show.

Krampus arrived in boundless variations, too many to name, too many to count; some with two horns, some with four, some with more than four. The horns, smooth or ribbed, branched out in endless configurations from wooden masks and headpieces. In shaggy costumes and pointed ears, covered in clanging metal, and wielding sticks and branches and fine wooden whisks, their horrific visages deeply shadowed in the light of the torches and flares and lanterns they carried, the hordes of the dark lord Krampus arrived in the streets of Bad Mitterndorf, bidding ill omen to all.

Bobby glanced over his shoulder and was not surprised to see the Gray Man and Uncle Oskar had vanished, eaten by the darkness and the crowd; their remains hidden perhaps somewhere beneath the stray flakes of winter.

Krampus in a white mask and a black mien, with a band around its middle and large metal balls on its bent back, howled like a wolf. Krampus with six horns and bristly black fur, raged at Bobby, brandishing a switch of birch rods. Krampus, red-faced with whited-out eyes and hugely oversized ram's horns, on a float, played a drum solo with glow sticks.

Spectators laughed, chanted, screamed, and growled, and Bobby felt his sense of identity slipping away as he tentatively joined in the crowd's abandon.

Soon he was whooping and cheering wholeheartedly as Krampus on a motorcycle gunned the engine and popped a wheelie. As Krampus in a crate-like shamble of a wooden vehicle, threatened the crowd with long, yellow teeth and claw gloves. As a hanged Krampus danced delightedly from a gibbet on wheels.

Bobby cheered the anarchy, wishing all the world would spin from its axis. That up would become down, and the debris of civilization would rain on them all like snow in an upended glass globe. He wanted things to go more and more terribly wrong. In his heart, he yearned for nothing less than the downfall of every nation on the planet.

The street brimmed with smoke from the dozens of billowing flares waved and held aloft by Krampus in all its deviations: lurching Krampus, brawling Krampus, Krampus with the flapping leather tongue. One pulled off a woman's knit beanie and made her jump to get it back. Another whacked with a stick through a gap in the fence, stinging a spectator's leg. This one in fighting stances. That one with a nose ring, rattling the thick chains around its neck. Others, deliriously roughhousing with the crowd and with one another in a glorious orgy of wildness and abandon.

Then, from the turmoil and smoke appeared a silhouette out of nowhere, like a horror from a nightmare, massive and miscreant and moving toward Bobby in measured strides, it's limbs clicking puppet-like at its joints, its cylindric, bell-shaped head lolling almost merrily. As it stepped from the smoke, hideous details of it countenance appeared: feral, curled horns that crossed at their tips; sly golden eyes, iridescent and mesmerizing; talon-like teeth and cloven hooves. Part goat, part demon, its shaggy, lice-infested fur a blood-streaked reddish brown. Its long, pointed tongue searching out Bobby in the crowd.

"Krampus is a wicked creature who comes after children who misbehave," Uncle Oskar had said. *"Bad children."*

The creature beckoned him with one clawed hand. Beckoned him into the street, into the smoke, into the very jaws of chaos.

Bobby felt his body being commandeered by a higher source. Some inner part of him was taking leave. It was the part he required to keep his mind from jumping the tracks, from melting and dissolving into a puddle of sludge. Gone was this failsafe he'd carried since the grisly day of his parents' massacre, and with it, all restraint. All resistance.

"Y-yes," Bobby stammered, hopping the fence. "T-this is where I belong. This is my home." His eyes watered from the smoke.

Krampus the punisher, horrific and hateful, glared down at him, but Bobby was unafraid.

Even as the biting whip flayed his skin. Even as the claws ripped gouts of blood from his veins. Even as the long, yellow teeth mauled at the crown of his head. He gave himself to this creature, willingly, until there was little physical left to give.

Then Krampus held open his sack, and from its black innards came the sounds of children, some giggling, some weeping for their mothers.

Bobby took one last look back before climbing in.

From the pandemonium that was the crowd shined the steely gleam of the Gray Man's eyes.

The Whispering Wings
of the Bat

"The sun is set; the swallows are asleep;
The bats are flitting fast in the gray air."
—Percy Bysshe Shelley, "Evening: Ponte Al Mare, Pisa"

T o be honest, I barely remember my Great Aunt Glendoline. She was never one for family gatherings. We met at a funeral visitation once—for my Uncle Donnie, I think it was—but I was only about twelve at the time, and the memory's hazy.

My mother introduced us: "Glendoline, this is your nephew Holden. Holden, this is my big sister Glendoline from New Hope."

I remember wearing this new suit with a collar that felt like it was made out of cardboard. It kept chafing the back of my neck. "How do you do?" I inquired, shaking Aunt Glendoline's hand, which was mostly just skin on bone.

"I'm fine, young man." She looked too old to be Mom's sister, but when she smiled, she had Mom's twinkle in her eyes. "It's a pleasure to meet you."

I said it was a pleasure for me, as well, and hurried off to join my friend David at the vending machines.

As I later learned, Aunt Glendoline was something of a big deal among bat conservators, though my parents had hardly mentioned this before. But after Uncle Donnie's funeral, Mom dug up an old copy of *National Geographic* magazine with a story about Glendoline Price, "the bat woman of Minnesota." There was even a photo of her shielding her eyes as she looked into a twilight sky filled with hundreds of bats.

According to the article, which was about fifteen years old, Aunt Glendoline had helped trace migratory patterns of frog-eating bats at Barro Colorado Island in Panama, and had studied vampire bats in Chiapas, Mexico. She'd clambered into bat caves in—among other places—Ecuador, Brazil, Cuba, American Samoa, Thailand and Kenya.

Noting that bats gave most people the willies, the magazine went on to say the little creatures were actually quite beneficial: "A single bat can catch and devour a thousand insects in sixty minutes. The bats from just one cave could eat over a hundred tons of bugs in a night. In addition, bats pollinate flowers and dispense plant seeds, playing a key role in reforesting African savannas and South American rainforests."

Some bats were even friendly-looking, especially the pups, with fuzzy, foxlike faces and big hazel eyes. The magazine had a photo of one of these, looking like a cuddly, stuffed toy you'd win at a carnival.

This was all interesting to me as a red-blooded American twelve-year-old.

My dad, though, thought the idea of conserving bats was looney. "If a bat bites you, you get rabies," he said. "Why monkey around with animals that can kill you?"

Later I learned that the chance of getting rabies from bats was miniscule. Less than one percent of the creatures carry the disease, and the odds of getting bit by a bat, even a diseased one, are smaller yet. Still, those who handle bats regularly wear leather gloves and are vaccinated against rabies just to be safe. And people should steer clear of bats active during the daytime and ones that don't fly well. Otherwise, they generally won't bother you if you don't bother them.

Bats became the topic of my Science Fair project that year, and I became reasonably well-versed in various species common to Minnesota, especially the big brown bat. However, my fascination with the animals turned out to be short-lived and was soon replaced with interests in girls, cars, and video games.

Aunt Glendoline's name hardly ever came up again until years later when Covid 19 struck her down. She was in North Memorial Hospital in Robbinsdale, and we couldn't even visit her due to Covid restrictions. At her funeral, only Mom and Dad and Mom's brother, Uncle Ralph, were allowed to attend. Poor Aunt Glendoline was just another one of the million or so U.S. victims of that deadly plague.

Her estate consisted of nearly a half-million dollars in stocks and bonds, and her house in New Hope. At first, they planned to sell the house and divide the profits equally, then Uncle Ralph suggested they split the cash and give the house to me, since I was the only one in the family without a place of my own. Uncle Ralph always was a generous man.

My parents agreed. They all met with the lawyers and settled the estate.

There was just one hitch, though: Aunt Glendoline's dying wish was that whoever took possession of the place had to keep the bat houses she'd posted in her backyard. Since I knew bats were basically harmless, I accepted this stipulation. And just like that, I'm a homeowner.

THE NEIGHBORHOOD, on New Hope's west side, was a mix of retirees, blue-collar types, young professionals, and middle-aged civil servants; a racial hodgepodge but mostly white and largely the type of people who kept to themselves. It was a quiet place with older one- and two-story houses. Aunt Glendoline's home was a baize ranch house with a fair-sized front lawn, a two-car garage, and a backyard enclosed in a privacy fence.

"What do you think?" I asked my girlfriend, Marla, after I'd pulled the old-but-still-decent-looking Saturn into the driveway for the first time.

"Looks nice," she said. "Let's see what it looks like inside."

I'd been living with Marla for two years then, in a one-bedroom apartment on St. Claire Avenue in St. Paul. A quaint, garden-level rental, within walking distance of stores, restaurants, and coffeehouses, we liked living there well enough (aside from having to deal with a few rowdy tenants), but we were nearing that point in a relationship where we felt the need to decide on whether to go all in, commitment-wise, or maybe go our separate ways. I know, everyone doesn't have to get married, but I'd always thought I would eventually, and so did she. And with the move and the house, it seemed like everything was coming to a head.

Marla and I met one night at the Minnesota Music Café in St. Paul, a club with a large dance floor where many local bands played. That night, the group was Jonah and the Whales, an up-tempo rock band featuring a female lead singer. When the band broke into a thundering cover of Simon and Garfunkel's "Cecilia," I asked Marla to dance, and we'd pretty much been together ever since.

Aunt Glendoline's place—no, check that—Holden and Marla's new place hadn't been gone through since Aunt Glendoline died, and stepping into the expansive living room was almost surreal, like stepping into a somewhat eccentric stranger's house. It smelled of potpourri and scented candles, and though generally tidy, cobwebs collected in the corners, and neat stacks of magazines and paperwork covered every available surface. A large bookcase dominated one wall, and another featured framed photos of bats in the wild. A woven throw rug in a geometric pattern lay in the middle of a solid wood floor, while glass-topped lamp tables squatted at either end of a charcoal-colored, contemporary sofa. A tan, corduroy lounge chair set off to one side looked like no one had ever sat in it.

I stood there a minute, the brass keys to the home cool in my hands.

"What do you think?" I asked Marla again.

"Not too shabby."

Marla was a long-necked, long-legged woman of Swedish descent in her early thirties. She wore her blond hair in a sort of boxy, sixties style, and usually shunned makeup and jewelry. In clothing, her tastes ran toward the conservative, but she wasn't shy about showing off her legs. She worked in human resources at the Best Buy headquarters in Richfield, and liked her job well enough. The employee discount was generous, and she'd held down her job a sufficient time to build up a decent salary.

Me, I was a little older and worked as foreman at a printing plant that specialized in funeral cards. We had longstanding relations with local mortuaries, and business was steady in good economies and bad, though things slowed a bit during Covid restrictions. The pay was so-so, but working conditions were great. I'd been there five years.

"Let's check out the other rooms," I suggested.

The rest of the house was on par with the living room: modern with quaint touches to give it a lived-in feel. The tank lid on the toilet, for instance, sported a macramé cover, and potpourri and candles were present in every room. The bed was only queen-sized, but was one of those adjustable types that let each side be contoured to the shape favored by the individual sleeper, which Marla just loved. Both sides of the bed had been adjusted to exactly the same shape, which led us to believe Aunt Glendoline generally slept solo. A guest bedroom gathered dust, and a fourth room overflowed with boxes, telling us we had some major cleanup ahead. The kitchen appliances were newer, and everything appeared to be in working order. The kitchen table, which had four chairs but could easily seat six, again held neat stacks of papers and magazines and a pair of high-powered binoculars.

A large window looked out on a backyard dappled in August sunshine: a towering maple tree, night sky petunias and jasmine, and grass overlong and in need of cutting. Along the rear fence were a dozen rectangular bat houses that betrayed no signs of habitation other than some guano splatterings on the ground. The bats would probably be snoozing inside their homes this afternoon. I could picture Aunt Glendoline peering at the roosts through her binoculars at dusk, waiting for the little creatures to take flight.

Marla's parents, who lived in rural Crookston, had taught her to fear bats, but she promised to keep an open mind.

"After all, we have to get along with our new neighbors," she said, indicating the bat houses with her chin.

"I promise you," I said, "you won't even know they're here."

WE KEPT MOST of Aunt Glendoline's furniture because it was much better than ours, which we'd accumulated mainly from garage sales and thrift stores. All I personally wanted was that corduroy lounge chair, which featured a vibrating mode that soothed my lower back, an area of recurring discomfort inflamed by the necessity of moving heavy boxes of paper at the print shop.

I told Marla that, as far as I was concerned, the rest of the furniture was hers. "Just let me have this chair though," I begged. *"Please."*

69

She agreed to this on the condition that I be the one to get rid of the stacks of Aunt Glendoline's papers in the living room. This took much longer than I anticipated because I kept being drawn into the papers' contents, most of which featured information on various megabats, a topic that Aunt Glendoline appeared to be zeroing in on when the Covid hit her.

For instance, I learned from these documents that the giant golden-crowned flying fox of the Philippines was believed to be the largest and rarest of all bats. Weighing as much as three pounds and with a wingspread upwards of five feet, golden-crowned flying foxes got their name from the color of their fur, which runs gold from between their eyes to the napes of their necks. Existing chiefly on figs, the golden-crowned flying fox was endangered, and one variant—the Panay flying fox—was already sadly extinct. Several papers on the creatures by bat biologists, accompanied by photos, made up multiple stacks.

When I told Marla about the giant golden-crowned flying fox, she made a face. "Too bad Aunt Glendoline didn't study puppies or bunny rabbits."

Our first days in the new house were hectic. Neither of us could afford to take time away from our jobs, so between working, moving, cleaning, and otherwise settling in, our time was pretty well filled.

We were in the place for almost two weeks before the pace slowed to a manageable level, and we decided to have my mom and dad over for dinner.

"So, how are you getting along with your hairy homeys?" Dad asked Marla at the kitchen table, motioning with his head toward the backyard.

Marla swallowed a mouthful of her eggplant lasagna and shrugged. "We haven't even seen one, so far. If we run into one, Holden says he'll protect me."

Dad chuckled. He always liked Marla. Mom, on the other hand, was still on the fence about her.

"Stake through the heart," Dad said, squinching his nose in a way that lifted his aviator eyeglasses toward his brow. "Only way to deal with the flying rats."

Marla smiled. "This is strictly a cruelty-free zone," she said. "We won't be stabbing any bats around here."

"Well, you could take down those awful bat houses, anyway," he said.

Mom pursed her lips. "Now, Roger, that's not even fair. You know Glendoline wanted those houses to stay." She glared at him, red-faced, letting him know she meant business.

He showed her his palms. "I'm just saying, if those critter cages came down, who cares? Ralph isn't going to raise a ruckus. Are you?"

An uneasy silence fell.

I cleared my throat. "The bat houses stay, for now at least." Then, changing the topic, I asked my dad, "How do you think the Vikings will do this year under the new coach?"

His eyes rolled behind the aviator glasses. "About the same as they did under the old coach." And he launched into his rant on how General Manager Mike Lynne had destroyed the franchise for good with his ill-advised Herschel Walker trade, which happened all the way back in 1989. Dad could hold a grudge for a long time.

MOST OF THE DOCUMENTS Aunt Glendoline had collected in her neat piles went straight to the recycling plant, but a few interested me, and I kept them for later reading. For instance, one small stack was dedicated to the spectral bat (*Vampyrum spectrum*), a large, carnivorous bat that fed on birds, reptiles, amphibians, and small mammals—even other bats. Ultimately, I kept a Xerox paper box full of the items I planned to peruse, which I stored in the room with all of Aunt Glendoline's other boxes. Another week passed before I got around to examining my stash.

It was a chilly September evening and Marla was deep into one of her true-crime shows when I pulled out the box, made myself a cup of green tea, and settled into the corduroy lounge chair for a night of reading.

I'd been going through the papers for a half-hour or so, reading about the taxonomy and mating habits of the giant golden-crowned flying fox, the big-eared wooly bat, and the spectral bat when I came across a clipping from a Mexican newspaper. Though the article was in Spanish, an English translation was attached to it.

The headline read: Did Ghosts Chase Off the Residents of Misnebalam? Or Was It a Man-Eating Bat?

"Marla, listen to this."

She hit the pause button on *Dateline*. "Yeah?"

"For many years, historians and archeologists have debated why Misnebalam, in the Mexican state of Yucatán, became a ghost town. Some believe it was because the area's main crop, the fibrous henequén plant, was replaced in the 1950s by synthetic textiles. Some say a ghost named Juliancito haunted the town, scaring off the inhabitants. Others, including former resident Jesus Santiago, 78, claim the real reason Misnebalam became abandoned was the sudden appearance of a man-eating carnivore called the silver-backed jackal-headed bat."

"Hmmm," Marla said. "Is there such a thing as a man-eating bat?"

"Not that I've ever heard of. But according to this old Mexican dude, 'The bat is real. I have seen it. When I was just a boy, one appeared at our front window one night. It was huge and angry-looking, covered in course fur, with a long, black face; teeth like a jackal; and eyes like the devil. The middle finger of each paw was a talon or a claw. The bat was only at our window for an instant, but it has flown in my nightmares ever since.'"

"Hmmm. Has anyone else ever seen it?"

"It says here there have been reports of the silver back for more than a hundred years, but the old Mexican is the only one identified by name."

"Sounds like an urban legend."

"Maybe, but Aunt Glendoline thought enough of it to pay a visit."

Marla scratched at a knee, and frowned. "Your Aunt Glendoline went to Yucatán, Mexico, looking for man-eating bats? Seems a little bizarre, even for the bat woman. Did she find any?"

I shrugged. "If she did, she didn't mention it in these papers. But here's a copy of her grant request showing Yucatán, Mexico, as the destination. It's dated four years ago. Says she planned to study a rare species of carnivore bat. My guess is it was the silver back."

Marla's features expressed disbelief. "I'm turning *Dateline* back on," she said, thumbing the remote.

But I could tell she was more bothered by the article than she let on.

IT WAS AROUND THIS TIME. Marla began complaining of chills, headaches, and stiffness in her joints. She developed a dry cough and ran a slight fever. At first, she treated it as a cold, with acetaminophen and fluids. Just to be safe, she took a home Covid test, which came up negative. Determined to soldier on, she tried downplaying the significance of the symptoms, until one night she showed me reddish bumps on her lower leg.

"You might want to have a doctor look at that," I suggested.

The next day, she did.

Calling me at work from the Health Partners Clinic in St. Louis Park, she said, "The doctor thinks I may have a fungal infection. Invasive aspergillosis, she called it."

"Fungal? You mean mold?"

"Yeah, but we're not sure whether I got it from our new house or if it's from work. They're doing some remodeling in the lunch room, and that's probably where it's coming from. Some of that food has been in the cupboards and refrigerator for eons. Anyway, the doctor says it's nothing to worry about. She's sending me home with some medicine and says, if it doesn't clear up in a week or so, I should get a CAT scan and some blood tests."

That night, we walked through the house, including the basement, searching for patches of mold. We found none, though the room jammed with boxes could have hidden some. But, aside from a few cobwebs, it looked spotless.

"Let's just keep this room's door closed," I suggested. "Just to be safe."

Marla agreed.

In coming days, the medicine the doctor had given her proved useless. Her symptoms not only remained but grew worse. She coughed more frequently, and she began having shortness of breath. When she started sweating profusely and complaining of chest pain, I brought her to the emergency room at Maple Grove Hospital, and she soon signed in as a patient.

After mulling over test results, a sharp-featured doctor with a bristly moustache entered her room, carrying a clipboard. By then, it was nearly midnight, and Marla was fast asleep.

"You the husband?" he asked.

"Fiancé," I said.

"Well, your betrothed has an acute case of histoplasmosis. It's a lung infection caused by bird or bat feces.

"Bat?"

"Yes. Bird or bat. If the source is your home, you probably have it as well, but not severely enough to provoke symptoms. It usually requires exposure to quite a lot of it to trigger reactions as severe as hers."

A dread sunk in me. "We have some bat houses in the back yard. My aunt used to study bats. Do you think they could be the cause of Marla's sickness?"

The doctor crossed the arm with the clipboard across his chest and stroked his chin. "I wouldn't think so, but neither would I risk it. She could be highly sensitive to the disease. I'd take down those bat houses as soon as possible, and clean up any residual droppings. Also, search the exterior of your house for cracks where bats may be getting in. They don't need much of an opening to squeeze through. Do you have an attic?"

"Not sure. There doesn't seem to be an entryway to one. At least not one that we've found."

"Well, I'd search a little more thoroughly. Sometimes closets will have false ceilings that open on the attic. Have you heard any scratching noises or cheeps?"

I shook my head. "Nothing."

"Well, the attic could be well insulated, which might keep in the noise. Just to be safe, if you don't find a way in, you may want to punch a hole in the ceiling. If you do find bats, I'd call an exterminator."

"But she's going to be alright?"

"I'm confident she'll make a full recovery."

He patted my shoulder, then excused himself to continue his rounds.

Bat guano? Could that be the culprit?

The thought was enough to give even a bat enthusiast the shivers.

MARLA AWOKE the next morning, still a little groggy with sickness, but the sweating had ceased, and she had a bit more color in her face.

"How do you feel?" I asked, straightening up in the hospital chair beside her bed where I'd spent the night. I yawned and stretched and rose to my feet.

"Like a freight train just ran through my skull." She paused, looking around and plucking at her tongue as if trying to remove a hair. "What did the doctors say?"

I poured her a cup of water from a pitcher on her bedside tray and told her everything.

She gave me a curious look. "Bat shit, huh?" She sipped from her water cup. "I thought you said bats were harmless."

"They usually are."

She tapped her teeth thoughtfully on the rim of her cup, then said, "Well, you'd better figure out what to do about this because I'm not going back to that house until I know it's safe."

Who could blame her?

When we checked out of the hospital, Marla arranged to stay with a coworker who lived in nearby Crystal. I dropped her off, feeling a tug at my heart, and drove back to the house.

Among Aunt Glendoline's bat gear was a pair of thick, leather gloves and a butterfly net. I took these out to the back yard and cautiously approached the first bat shelter.

Although guano splattered the lower fence and the ground, it wasn't that much, and what was there looked like it had been there for a while. I tapped on the bat house, which was shaped somewhat like a deep letterbox that opened on the bottom, and listened for movement, but there was none. Slowly, I took it down from the hook that held it in place, tilted the bottom opening skyward, and shook it. Nothing happened. I peered inside. *No bats.*

75

One by one, I repeated these steps with each bat house and got the same result each time. No fresh guano either. Well, it was early October. Maybe the bats migrated to a warmer clime. I collected the bat houses in plastic bags and hauled them off to the trash container in the garage.

I sprayed disinfectant on the guano, then walked around the house, looking for places bats could get in but found nothing suspicious.

Finally, backing up, I noticed a vent at the roof's peak that appeared to be open on the sides. There was probably a screen inside it to keep animals out, but I knew I had to check to be sure.

I'm not big on heights, and the idea of crawling around on a roof did not exactly fill me with joy, but I had to do it, so I decided to do it quickly and get it over with.

The early October wind was strong enough to keep my nerves on edge as I clambered over shingles on all fours and made my way to the roof vent. Inside, it was as I might have expected: the vent's screen was knocked out, leaving a black opening to the attic big enough for a squirrel to pass through.

By the time I'd taken my measurements, went to the Home Depot on Boone Avenue, returned, and installed the new vent, it was nearing dusk. The new vent was a fourteen-inch, externally braced, turbine type. I added extra screws to tighten the fit at the base, then caulked around it. No way any critters were getting through that.

I detailed my progress to Marla over the phone that evening.

"Sounds like you've accomplished a lot," she said. "Did you find a way into the attic in the house?"

"Not yet. I'm doing that after work tomorrow. Don't want to exhaust all the fun in one day." Truth was, I was dead tired. I'd gotten little sleep, then was busy all day. About all I had left was the strength to bake a Daiya frozen pizza and curl up in bed for a little light reading.

I browsed some more of Aunt Glendoline's documents and came across an interesting fact. Carnivorous bats, apparently, were unlike other carnivores in that they don't tear with their teeth, they swallow their prey whole, bones and all. But if silver backed, jackal-headed bats really existed and really did eat people, they would have to rip off chunks, wouldn't they? *So, there's a pleasant thought.*

Setting the alarm for seven a.m., I turned off the light and floated off to sleep, my subconscious crawling with thoughts of flesh-eating bats.

I DREAMT that I was walking through a cathedral when a noise above me caught my attention. The basilica's massive walls echoed with a rustling sound.

I started to look up when a woman ran into me, nearly upending me, screaming and slapping at her head. A giant golden-crowned flying fox was entangled in her hair; long, leathery wings beating at either side of her face. *Was that Marla's mother?*

"Help me!" she shrieked. But before I could react, she'd run down the main aisle, off into thick shadows beyond the altar, and was gone.

I looked toward the rafters and saw something moving up in the dark.

Just then, my father walked up to me, baby bats squirming out of the sleeves and collar of his shirt, dropping to the ground in a seemingly endless stream.

"Dad, are you alright?"

He rolled eyes behind his aviator glasses. "Stake through the heart," he said. "Only way to deal with the flying rats."

Then he, too, was gone.

Something caused the light to shift through the cathedral's stained-glass windows, and I could now see a smudge of white in the darkness overhead. I was squinting at it when it became unattached from the rafters and dropped heavily through the darkness to the floor beside me.

"Marla?"

Yes, it was Marla, stark naked and squealing at me, her fingernails preternaturally long and pointed, her teeth fanged and snapping. She wanted to bite me, I could tell. I was both frightened and aroused by the sight of her.

"You did this to me," she said in barks and squeals.

She leapt menacingly toward me, but before she could reach me, she and the cathedral evaporated into mist.

A huge banging sound had cut through my dream, and I was suddenly awake and alert.

The noise came from the kitchen.

I sat up in bed and listened.

"Who's there?" I called.

No answer.

I turned on the light and searched for some weapon, but all I could find was the butterfly net I'd planned to use earlier at the bat houses. I grabbed it by the handle and skulked out my bedroom door.

A whispering sound swept through the house.

As I made my way down the hallway to the living room, I felt a sudden breeze overhead, and caught just a flash of motion. By then, the kitchen light switch was closest. I reached into the kitchen and turned on the ceiling light.

For an instant, the brightness blinded me.

Then, in the light that limned the living room, I saw nothing but a suspiciously crooked lampshade.

The kitchen, however, was a mess. Screws and metal panels were strewn across the floor. My teapot was also on the floor, overturned, and leaking water. Over the stove, a dented fan dangled from a wire. I looked up into open space where the stove's exhaust venting had been and saw a profound darkness that reached all the way to *the attic!*

Something sufficiently big and powerful had broken free of the attic through the exhaust duct. Of course! When I'd installed the roof turbine, I'd blocked the only exit. I thought I was keeping bats out, but really, I'd trapped something in.

Still clutching the butterfly net, I proceeded through the living room into the hall, listening for the whisper of wings.

I flipped the light switch to the bathroom, but that room was empty. Next, I came to the bedroom, turned on the lights, and looked around. Nothing. Same thing with the guest room.

That left the storage room, still filled with Aunt Glendoline's boxes. The door was partially open. I trudged toward it, feeling lightheaded. I knew I had to turn on this room's light as well, but I dreaded doing it, certain it was going to reveal something I did not want to face.

My trembling hand found the light switch, and I flipped it.

A tower of boxes smashed to the floor, and rushing through the air toward me came the most gargantuan bat I had ever encountered, fibrous wings stretched more than four feet wide, black lips pulled taunt, showing sharp, slimy fangs through which it hissed at me.

I barely had time to step back, and when the bat flew past me, brawny wings slapped my left temple and arm, and I reeled.

The creature circled in the living room, then spun toward me, eyes demonic, razor teeth ready to shred me to pieces. I couldn't believe my eyes: the beast was a jackal-headed silver back. I was sure of it.

Aunt Glendoline must have brought one of the devils home from Mexico and kept it in her attic.

Though she no doubt left the bat with sufficient food to last a day or two, she hadn't counted on getting sick and dying. Driven mad with hunger, the silver back had burst through the screen on the roof vent, and had probably dined out on the smaller bats, maybe birds, maybe neighborhood cats. But this time, I could see from the glowering look directed my way, the creature had a bigger prey in mind.

I hunched over and raised the ridiculously inadequate butterfly net in a defensive posture.

The beast crashed into the net's flimsy aluminum frame, which dented but held well enough to deflect the attack. Again, the leathery wings raked my face, and I felt the scrape of a clawed digit on one cheek. I whirled in time to see the bat bounce off a wall and flutter to the floor.

Scrambling to the living room with my damaged net, I twisted at the front door's handle. I could hear the silver back's wings take flight behind me as I frantically tugged the doorknob. The inner door slammed open, and I reached for the outer screen just as searing pain tore through my shoulder. The bat, now firmly affixed to the back of my neck, had sunk those razor teeth into my left bicep and was attempting to make a meal of me.

Thinking quickly, I flung myself to the ground, left side first. The silverback struggled to get free and managed to do so clumsily as I hit the floor.

The pain from my wounded arm hitting the carpet flashed through my upper body. It felt like a spear tearing into me. I rolled onto my back and tried getting up, but the jackal-headed bat lit on my chest, and my elbows collapsed as the beast cheeped angrily at me, inches away, the wicked teeth red with my blood and reeking of past carrion consumed. I swear the silverback leered at me.

The clawed digits ripped into my sternum as the creature lunged for my face.

I managed to get my head turned in time to avoid it becoming a target, but to my horror, I felt the eager fangs chewing on my earlobe.

I rose on my shoulder blades, rocked my torso, kicked out wildly, rocketing the screen door open and bursting it from its top hinges. Giddy, almost delirious with fear and adrenaline, I grabbed and squeezed the bat's furry body with all my remaining strength, and yanked. The flesh of my chest rent open as the silverback's claws tried unsuccessfully to maintain their grip.

Pitching the creature outward, I watched dizzily as the silverback clipped the top corner of the open screen door and sailed off into the night.

The open door let in a wintry October breeze that felt soothing on my bloody and sweaty skin. I'm not sure how long I lay there. I'm not sure how time is even measured when you've just narrowly escaped a horrible fate. Let's say, a while.

EVENTUALLY, I FOUND MY FOOTING, closed the inner door, and stumbled to the bathroom. The light was still on.

Leaning on the bathroom sink in front of the mirror, I examined my lacerations.

My ear looked bad, but when I wiped away the blood with a washcloth, I could see the lobe was mangled but still largely intact. Pulling off the T-shirt that had served me as a pajama top, I wiped the wounds on my chest and arm, and could see they were more serious. About a half-inch of skin and muscle had been torn from my left bicep, and the chest gashes would require stitches to heal properly. I patched myself up as best I could with gauze and bandages.

Still shaken, and listening attentively for any further sounds of wings or squealing, I made my way to the bedroom closet, where I slid into a loose-fitting, poplin shirt and buttoned it up high enough to hide the dressing on my chest wounds.

It was almost sunup, and I knew I had work to do before heading to the emergency room at Maple Grove Hospital.

I made a cup of green tea, heating it in the counter microwave oven. Then, retrieving my toolbox, I went to work on the stove's exhaust fan, bending some of the metal hood parts back into shape, fitting in the dangling fan and the screened covering, and replacing the screws. It would take a close inspection to notice anything amiss with the vent. I sipped the last of the coffee in the mug and prepared a fresh cup.

Putting away the tools, I made the rounds of the house, restacking the tumbled boxes in the storage room and turning off all the lights.

Then I went to the garage, fired up the Saturn, and drove to the hospital. I already had my story constructed. I'd been attacked this morning by a dog—a sleek and powerful Doberman pinscher, gray with cropped ears—on my front lawn. That's what I told the doctor, my boss at the print shop, and my girlfriend, Marla, when I called her.

"When it rains, it pours," she said.

Back at the house, I eventually found the false ceiling that allowed entry to the attic. It was in a back closet of the storage room. How Aunt Glendoline climbed up there, I'll never know. But with one peek, I could see there was too much guano caked on the attic floor for me to remove.

So, I hired environmental cleaners, and it took them the better part of a day to scrape and sanitize the room. They hauled off trash bags of bat feces and wads of soiled insulation. They fumigated the attic, and the smell of the fumigant hung around for a few days, but eventually it disappeared, and, at last, I retrieved Marla from her friend's house.

She never knew about the night the jackal-headed silverback emerged from the kitchen and attacked me. I never told anyone. Let's face it: who'd believe me? And even if they did, what could be done about it now? And, truthfully, I was *afraid* to let anyone know. I pictured a pandemonium of police and media and angry neighbors invading our life. Our names and the name of the esteemed bat biologist

Glendoline Price would be dragged through the mud, and to what purpose?

Still, I often wondered whatever happened to that bat after it flew off into the night. Depending on the species, bats can live upwards of 25 years. Maybe it migrated to a warmer climate. Maybe it stayed in Minnesota and was destroyed by the bitter cold of the winter.

That October there were many reports of house pets disappearing on the west side of New Hope. Police suspected thieves of selling the pets to testing labs, but no one was ever captured in connection with the crimes. As far as I know, there were no reports of people in New Hope being bitten by a bat. Certainly not eaten.

As far as I know.

Home Again

"'Home is the place where, when you have to go there,
They have to take you in.'"
—Robert Frost, "The Death of the Hired Man"

I f you're from Minnesota, you probably already know about the
snowfall of '91. The Great Halloween Blizzard, they call it. Two
inches of snow were predicted that day, but you know what they
say about economists and meteorologists—the old take-their-
forecasts-with-a-pinch-of-salt admonition. Anyway, anyone believing
weather prophets that day was in for a shock.

The flakes started falling about 11:30 a.m. Thursday in the Twin
Cities. It was closer to one o'clock in Duluth. By 4 p.m., the freeways
around Minneapolis were slicker than snot on linoleum, and the field of
visibility was rapidly shrinking. Cars piled up in ditches, Metro Transit
buses fishtailed, and snowplows fought a losing battle. That day, eight
inches accumulated. The State Patrol reported more than 400 crashes.
Trick-or-treaters largely sulked.

It snowed through the night and all day Friday, the white stuff
piling up another twenty inches that, all told, snapped a state record for
snowfall in a twenty-four-hour period. Most schools and businesses
shut down, snowblowers and shovels worked overtime, and hospitals
were kept busy attending to frost burns, twisted ankles, and numerous
other weather-related mishaps. Eighty-thousand people lost electricity.
The governor declared a state of emergency.

The storm officially became a blizzard on Saturday, when temps dropped below zero and the winds began gusting up to sixty miles an hour.

Much was made of the tenacity of hardy Minnesotans, who shoveled out their fellow citizens, as well as themselves. Snow-removal crews earned their pay and most schools and businesses reopened by Monday morning. But the storm cost the state's economy something like $12 million, and some rural areas were still digging out past Wednesday.

And, oh, yeah, the Great Halloween Blizzard directly claimed at least twenty lives. Unfortunately, one of them was Henry Beekman's.

Henry, you see, had the misfortune of having retreated that particular Halloween Thursday to a lakehouse in the Northwoods of rural Puposky, far down a gravel road that quickly became unpassable, miles from the nearest neighbor.

HENRY KIDDED HIMSELF that he was only returning to the home of his youth to nurse poor health. The truth was that, although he did feel the mounting decrepitude of late middle-age sinking in, his health was the least of his losses. There was the added loss of his job, the loss of his wife, and the loss of his father, all of which were far more pressing than his trivial aches and sorenesses.

Loser, loser, loser. The Old Man had always said that Henry was nothing but a loser. Looked like fortune was proving him right.

The lakehouse was as Henry remembered it. The rambling rambler, the Old Man had called it: one story, long and expansive, due mostly to one-room annexes tacked on over the years by Henry's grandfather, who was an excellent carpenter, and later by the Old Man, who was not. Henry recalled a childhood of watching his father saw wooden boards, pound nails, and apply patches along ceiling and wall seams that were forever failing to keep out leaks.

Most of the furnishings predated Henry; many even the Old Man. Some, even predated Grandfather. The fixtures were not so much rustic (in the woodsy way the furniture in country homes tend to be) as they were remnants from another age, collected long ago by his mother and grandmother from antique shops for pennies on the dollar of what their going worth would be today. Especially noteworthy examples graced the entryway, where sat the oak dresser with its finishings cast from molten brass and its screwheads cut by Colonial hands with a hacksaw; and the living room, where the floral-patterned wing-backed sofa, faded and worn, looked every day it's two-hundred years; in the master bedroom with its walnut chifforobe with inlaid beveled mirror; and, of course, the kitchen, where four of the original six French table chairs with largely intact straw seats and still-firm joints gathered around the dining table. Other lesser treasures, too numerous to list, ornamented throughout the old house.

As a boy, his mother had warned him to take care around her antiques. Even now, he felt hesitant to touch them, the lessons of childhood having taken deep root.

His first impression on entering the lakehouse that day was that it needed a good airing out. The stuffiness was almost oppressive. No one had been in the place since the Old Man had died here over three months ago. Luckily, a Meals on Wheels driver had discovered him then. Otherwise, the old guy might still be here, stewing in the juices of decomposition. Stinking the joint up.

Henry set his bags beside the wing-backed sofa, stepped to the kitchen, and cranked open a window. Over the lake, clouds gathered in preparation for the coming snowfall, though Henry, of course, was expecting only a few inches. The opening let in a burst of icy air. Outside the window, a rusty temperature gauge, fashioned like a cartoon rooster, read twenty degrees. Almost tepid for a Minnesota late October.

In his childhood, Henry never let a day go by without checking the old rooster thermometer. Already, he felt himself slipping into ancient rites.

He walked through the rambling rambler, peeking into rooms, reacclimating himself to the place. Judging by the accumulated dust and cobwebs, some of these rooms hadn't been entered since he'd left thirty-some years ago.

There was the pantry, stocked with murky Mason jars of pickles and tomatoes canned by his mother before she died. There was the toilet, proudly installed by Grandfather some years before Henry's father was born and still containing the original porcelain throne. There was the master bedroom, the king-size bed a tangle of blankets and sheets, a stack of pillows with an impression of the Old Man's head, and the mirrored chifforobe, still retaining clothes from both of his parents.

Then there was the utility room. The dreaded utility room. Pulling the chain on the chamber's naked bulb lit a Kenmore washer and drier, an ancient furnace, a hot-water heater, brooms, mops, a Hoover vacuum cleaner, two rusty window air conditioners they'd used in the summers, and, in the corner, the stool where he'd sat—often in the dark—during time outs, whether he deserved them or not. Sometimes the Old Man would forget about him and leave him in the utility room for hours.

Or maybe the Old Man had left him in here intentionally. Henry could never be sure.

Elsewhere, the walls of his room (he still thought of it as his) bore cellophane-tape stains from the posters and pennants he'd posted in his youth. The shelves were empty, except for a broken model of a B-52 bomber. The closet and dresser still held old clothes from various stages of his life.

Mother's hobby room, of course, was locked. That was where she kept her sewing things, her knitting needles, and scrapbooking materials. At least, that's what she'd always said was in there. As far back as he could remember, the room was always locked. Funny how the Old Man had still kept it locked, even all these years after Mother died. As far as Henry knew, the room and its contents had never been taken in by a human eye since then. The Old Man had kept it just as she left it: a museum of sorts, Henry imagined it. Mother's hobby room with its unyielding doorknob.

He passed it by.

There was the guest bedroom, furnished largely in anticipation of the sibling who had never arrived. Stella: in some ways, as tangible a presence as Henry and his parents had ever been.

There was the reading room with its overstuffed armchair and shelves of musty paperbacks, mostly potboiler mysteries with a sampling of vintage sci-fi thrown in; a game room taken up largely by a chipped ping-pong table, cracked boxes of board games stacked in a far corner; and room upon room of storage. His parents were never ones for throwing much away.

Ghosts of the past stirred the dust motes in these rooms and in the long, crooked corridor that connected them.

Tucked among cardboard boxes and abandoned knickknacks were stored recollections that came upon him with a start. Things he wanted to remember and things he did not. In many cases, things he'd long ago forgotten. Or wished he had.

Returning to the living room and his bags, he sensed another's presence. A ghost of the past, perhaps, reaching out to him from long ago.

Carla (that was his wife's name) had never been to this place since, by the time he met her, he and the Old Man were already hip-deep into their mutual estrangement.

"You wouldn't like it, anyway," Henry'd said to her. "It smells like fungus and stale lake water. It has this long, meandering hallway lined with cluttered rooms. It's like walking around in some creepy museum. Honestly, the place is something that might have been dreamt up H.P. Lovecraft."

Or Edgar Allan Poe: "The Fall of the House of Beekman."

Henry decided to take a shower.

He was standing under a flaccid stream of water, washing away the day's dirt and sweat, when he heard a noise.

Old houses make noises, he told himself, but still ...

He turned off the water and listened. There it was again: a soft and airy sound, like a breeze lisping through a canyon or the low-pitched coo of a sleepy infant. It came from the corridor outside the bathroom. From the living room?

He wrapped a towel around himself and padded down the hallway's flattened gray carpet. When he stepped into the living room, he felt a faint tug of fear in his belly.

"Hello?" he said. "Is someone there?"

He became suddenly aware that he was weaponless and all but nude in the middle of nowhere. What if there was someone here? Some home invader seeking shelter from the cold who thought the place was empty? Clearly, he did not believe a stranger was in the lakehouse with him or he would have armed himself with a knife from the kitchen at the very least.

Regardless, there was no one in the living room. He waited to see if there would be any more ethereal coos. There weren't. Not then, anyway.

Outside, the snowfall went from drifting flakes to a steady cascade.

WITHIN THE LAKEHOUSE WALLS, Henry had been conceived, learned to walk, did his schoolwork, and kissed his first girl: bowlegged Sharon Carter, a Native gal with doe-like eyes and skin the color of coffee with cream. For a brief time, he'd had a friend named Skip Wilkins, who lived in Bemidji and sometimes stayed overnight on weekends. Skip's family came from Pennsylvania, and because of the move and related issues, Skip had been held back a year. When he showed up, scrawny and rough-cut, and with his cowlick hair, as a transfer student in Henry's ninth-grade English class, the two became fast friends.

Once, he'd accidentally shot Skip in the leg with a BB pistol they'd thought was empty. Skip had howled and writhed and swore from the pain, but he didn't get mad at Henry. Skip didn't blame him for the affront, knowing his friend would never intentionally hurt him. Skip had a way of seeing through surface things to the greater truths beneath.

When Henry was fifteen, Skip and his family moved back to Pennsylvania. Henry took it hard. Through the years, from time to time, he'd find himself thinking about his boyhood pal, wondering whatever became of the boy from Pennsylvania who had been his best friend in the whole world. He never had another friend who meant as much to him as Skip did.

Then, shortly after Skip left, Henry's mother died from a bacterial infection in her bloodstream. That was the official cause of death, anyway. Everyone who knew her knew she'd been dying for years, wasting away, a morose and skeletal woman he hardly recognized anymore. She'd lost that second child when Henry was just six, and gave up on happiness after that. A girl, the child would have been. His memories from that day so long ago were fuzzy, but parts were clear. He remembered, for instance, looking up at a crooked horizon and seeing his mother sprawled in the snow at the foot of the sledding mound, dark crimson spreading from between her legs.

What fate stole from her left her a shell of her former self; he recognized that even as a very young boy. Henry always suspected she blamed him for the loss of the child, Stella, though she never openly accused him.

Now, fully dressed, he pulled on his faux-leather aviator jacket, wedged into his Chuck Taylor sneakers, and stepped past the Colonial dresser, out the front door, and into the biting cold. By then, the snowfall exceeded the four-inches mark and showed no sign of subsiding. Making matters worse, the wind was picking up, contributing to a creeping reduction in visibility.

He trudged along the driveway to the roadside mailbox, grabbed a fistful of frozen letters, and stuffed them in a jacket pocket. Yes, even those three months gone, like the Old Man, still received junk mail and bills.

His Chuck Taylors and the socks underneath were already getting wet, and the brutal chill that rode in from Canada was wicking rapidly through his jacket. He turned to head back to the lakehouse when a sudden bellow filled the air. Not a wolf's cry—a black bear's foghorn moan. But that was ridiculous. Why would a bear choose to awaken from hibernation and venture out into a frightful winter's day like this one? He paused to look down the road where the snow was thickest and just made out the shadowy form of a Northwoods bear galloping toward him. A second moan erupted.

He didn't wait around for a third, but hurried down the drive, and was quickly inside, shutting the door behind him.

From a side window, he could see where the driveway met the main road and, sure enough, barely ten seconds passed before six-hundred pounds of yowling mama black bear came hurtling out of the snow. The creature ran for dear life, as if her backside were ablaze, clawing up clods of snow as she raged down the road to be swallowed, once again, by the storm.

Pores filling with sweat, Henry peered after the bear into the snow for a good five minutes before feeling safe enough to step away from the window. In all his life, he'd never before seen such a sight.

Working his way back to the front door, he opened it wide enough to stick out his head.

The relentless snowfall continued to choke off visibility, but now, in the distance, something foreign clotted in the winter sky. He watched it spread and darken like an awesome stain in the storm, and as it grew, a sound emerged as if hundreds of rugs were being beaten by knotted ropes. Soon the noise rose to a deafening roar, accompanied by the screeches and hoots of wild creatures.

From out of the tumult, dipped into sight two great horned and feathered beasts with taloned feet extended as if ready to strike, the ovals of their huge eyes shining brightly, as if with fear. Owls. The first of hundreds of owls who tore through the frozen vapor overhead, crying out in dreadful warning.

Henry stepped past the threshold and stood gaping upward in awe.

He'd never before seen more than two owls gathered together. Now he was witnessing hundreds passing over the lakehouse in a steady stream of panicky flight.

Owls. Imagine that. He shook his head.

When the last of the flock vanished into the restless churn of the storm, he stood for several moments, wondering what all these fleeing animals could possibly portend.

Returning indoors, he shook off the cold, but not the haunting feeling that something in the air was seriously awry.

NIGHT CAME ON.

He fixed himself a cup of coffee and sat on the two-hundred-year-old sofa and watched the weatherman from the Alexandria TV station explain that some shift in the Canadian air currents had thrown a monkey wrench into earlier forecasts, and it now appeared the snowfall was far from ending. Anyone could've looked out the window and come to the same conclusion. Now, the weatherman said, he expected at least another six inches and predicted that a pickup in the winds would blow the whole mess into a full-throated blizzard by morning.

Oh, boy.

When a commercial started, Henry went off in search of a blanket. The cold radiated through the walls of the lakehouse, which had always been insufficiently insulated, and he wasn't sure how much heating oil was in the tank out back, so he avoided the temptation to jack up the thermometer, at least until he had a chance to check the fuel gauge. He'd do that tomorrow, having had his fill of outside excursions for the day.

He remembered seeing a quilt on the Old Man's messy bed, but, at first, he was hesitant to grab it. All personal possessions the Old Man guarded over jealously. He didn't like people touching his things, and the personal items he was required on occasion to share with others he did so grudgingly. So, it was hardly a stretch to picture the Old Man glaring at Henry with those interrogator eyes of his; those icy blue orbs that had tunneled like diamond-tipped drill bits so many times into Henry's skull. It wasn't difficult at all to imagine those eyes boring into him from every dark corner as he yanked the quilt from the Old Man's bed and hurried out of the room.

Sipping his tea, wrapped in the quilt on the sofa in the pale gleam of "Top Cops"—a TV series in which police officers discussed their most challenging cases—Henry grew drowsy. It was partly because of the show, partly because of the cold, and partly because of exhaustion brought on by the long drive from Plymouth and the day's bizarre events.

He might have changed the channel, but the only other broadcast the TV received was a public station, which tended to be a little too cultured for Henry's tastes. Besides, changing the channel would have involved standing up and walking across the room, neither of which he was—in the tender grip of lethargy—particularly inclined to do.

On TV, a policewoman recalled her faceoff with a gunman at a police station. "It was the last thing I expected," she said.

Henry's eyelids grew heavy.

The next thing he knew, the policewoman transformed into one of the owls he'd seen earlier fleeing the storm.

The owl eyed him curiously, then said from the TV screen, "What are you doing here, Henry?" Her voice reminded him of a Hanna-Barbara cartoon character. Wilma Flintstone? Jane Jetson?

"I've returned home to rest up," he said. "Lately, I've been feeling a little under the weather."

He awoke, startled, a wave of panic sweeping through him.

91

It took a second for it to sink in where he was, and when it did, the realization came in a gawdawful surge of mixed remembrances. In his mind, three voices unreeled. "It's not working, Henry," Carla had said simply. "Sorry, Henry, but I have some bad news for you," his foreman had said, pulling a long face for Henry's benefit and ushering him into the main office and closing the door. The third voice was on the phone: "Henry Beekman? This is Sheriff Tim McNeal calling from Puposky. I'm sorry to inform you that your father, Charles, has passed away."

Suddenly, he became aware of the cold. He was uncovered. The quilt must have slipped off him. He felt around on the sofa, and when he searched the living-room floor, he found only the half-emptied coffee cup. *Had I done something with it in my sleep?* It occurred to him that maybe he'd just dreamt of pulling the quilt from the Old Man's bed, but that hardly seemed possible. He arose and opened the master bedroom's door. Sure enough, there it was: on the bed, in the exact position he remembered it being in earlier. *Am I losing my mind?*

Again, he pulled the blanket off the bed, dragging it through the hallway to the living room. He was about to sit on the sofa when a noise from outside beckoned him. A scraping noise barely audible over the now howling wind. Dropping the quilt to the floor, he turned on the outside light, opened the front door, and stuck his head out. "Hello. Is there anyone there?"

The wind now whipped the still-falling snow into drifts that rattled the roof and the windows and the branches of surrounding trees. He peered into this misty wildness and glimpsed a gray figure on the road that passed his driveway. "Hello?"

A man appeared to be dragging something, putting his full back into it. A sack of some kind, huge and seemingly quite heavy.

Henry stepped out and approached the man cautiously through the snow.

"Are you alright?" he shouted. "Do you need some kind of help?"

The man with the enormous sack, Henry now saw, was old and disheveled, with a long, ragged beard and unusually thick eyebrows.

"There's something dangerous in the storm," the stranger called to him. "Can't you feel it?"

Henry psychically searched the swirling flakes and blackness. He did feel … something.

"Would you like to come inside?" Henry called back. "Warm up; ride out the weather. You're perfectly welcome."

The man never paused in pulling at the ponderous sack. "You could accompany me, if you like. You'd be safer on the road than you are in there. At least you'd have a chance."

"Why would I do that? It's cold and windy out here."

The stranger, straining against his burden, moved slowly from sight. "Cold's the least of your worries," he shouted. "But suit yourself. It's your funeral."

Soon he and his sack disappeared into the storm, and Henry was left alone staring after him. Some old kook, he told himself. Some sad character whose train—aided by the snowstorm—had cleared the rails for good.

He shuffled back to the doorway of his youth, and wasn't entirely surprised to see that the quilt was again nowhere in sight.

Maybe the stranger with the sack had the right idea. He vaguely wondered whether there wasn't some threat in the storm. Something beyond his comprehension.

Opening the door to the master bedroom, Henry saw the quilt once again in its original position on the Old Man's bed. This time, he left it there.

HE'D NEVER TOLD CARLA about his mother's miscarriage at the sledding mound. Following his parents' lead, he'd kept the whole incident bottled up. After all, keeping secrets was a Beekman family tradition, a lesson he'd been taught many times over the years. If you ignore something long enough, it's like it—*poof*—disappears. You could almost make yourself believe it never happened.

Smoothing out the past, stamping it into the ground: like trampling flat a snow fort.

The only person Henry had ever mentioned the accident to was Skip, that summer day down by the lake when they were throwing stones into the water. But then, Skip was an easy one to talk to. Skip never judged.

"Where did this happen?"

"In the back of the lakehouse. I was just six at the time. I'd built this great pile of snow, and slicked it down with water that quickly froze. I wanted to show her how good I was on the sled. Her fearless son. It was one of those American Flyer iron-rung sleds. You laid on your belly on these wooden slats and zoom, you were off like a shot. You could steer it, sort of. Jeeze, I loved that sled."

"How did she get hurt?"

This was the part of the secret he'd buried most deeply. "The hill was about four feet tall. At the top, it was maybe two by four. I climbed up it from the back. It ramped down gradually, but you built up a decent speed. Enough to shoot you off a good twenty or thirty feet. I was coming down the ramp when I hit a bump and lost control. I remember clipping her ankle. Pretty hard. Enough to knock her to the ground and upturn me and the sled. I remember that jolt of metal on her bone shivering through me, and the next thing you know, I'm sailing through the air, coming down hard enough to knock the wind from me. For a minute, I just laid there, blinking away stars from my vision."

Skip didn't say anything. Never even looked at him, content to plunk rocks in the lake as if he were listening to a Twins game on the radio.

"When I got up, she was lying there, looking confused. Sure, her ankle was skinned but that was the least of it. All this blood was coming from between her legs, and she looked up at me like she wasn't sure who I was. I'd never seen her look at me that way before. It was a Saturday, and the Old Man was still in his robe. I remember hurrying to the lakehouse and him peeling out the door in his slippers, running through the snow. In another context, it might have looked comical: him flopping through the snow in his flappy slippers, his old robe ballooning out behind him. But, instead, I had this feeling in my gut like I'd just swallowed a bowlful of goldfish, and they were swimming around inside me."

"It wasn't your fault," Skip said, still not looking at him.

"The Old Man helped her back to the lakehouse, to the bathroom. She left drippings of her blood in the hallway. Both of them completely ignored me. The bathroom door closed, and they were in there a long time. I could hear water running in the tub. Muffled voices. She was crying, and he was telling her it was alright. Finally, she came out kind of wobbly with this dazed look. She passed me like I was a piece of furniture. Through the now-open doorway, I could see the Old Man on his hands and knees, mopping bloody water from the floor with bath towels. I stood there, not sure what to do, what to say. Hell, I was just a little kid, and this was so far beyond me."

"Then what?"

"Then … nothing. I thought we would go to the doctor that day, but we never did. She sat on the sofa, just staring off. Not sure where the Old Man took the bloody towels; carried them off to the utility room, I guess. Then he made us some Campbell's tomato soup, and we sat on either side of her, watching TV. I don't remember what we were watching. Cartoons were over by then. Probably some fishing show. The three of us sat there, slurping our soup. No one said anything. No one ever mentioned it from that day forward. At least not around me."

Skip nodded, clapped Henry reassuringly on the shoulder, then tossed another stone into the water.

THE LAKEHOUSE TEMPERATURE plunged. Frost bloomed on the windows and crept up from the bottoms of the doors. The old rafters and the water pipes began protesting, and Henry's out-breaths became vapor that hung blue and ghostlike in the glow of the TV screen.

He no longer needed to trudge outside and check the fuel tank. Plain enough, it was empty.

He called the fuel-oil company, hoping against hope for a rush delivery, but the phone just rang and rang. Anyway, he knew in his sinking heart that the chance of getting a truck out to rural Puposky in the middle of a snowstorm was virtually nil, especially late at night. *I'll have to tough it out, at least for tonight. Son of a bitch.*

He considered calling someone else. Carla, maybe. But what good would that do?

"Hi, Carla. This is the husband you kicked to the curb. Remember me? Just letting you know that I stand a decent chance of freezing to death this evening, which would save you the expense of a divorce attorney. Toodles."

95

He shuffled down the hallway, searching for sweaters, coats, and blankets. He came upon an old space heater in one of the storage rooms and carried it and an armful of bedcoverings and clothing to the wing-backed sofa, where he built himself a nest. Plugging in the heater, he felt a sense of relief wash over him as the heater's elements turned orange and began kicking off a small but measurable wave of warmth. He rubbed his hands together in it.

Outside, the wind growled at him, and snow pelted the lakehouse's outer walls and roof until the whole place rattled on its foundation.

He settled into his cocoon, the warmth of the heater on his face, when something in the air shuddered. The lights went out. In the deluge outside, no doubt, a powerline had snapped from the weight of the snow, knocking out electricity for miles in all directions.

Oh, boy, he thought. *This just keeps getting better and better.*

THE OLD MAN, Henry knew, had always kept a flashlight in the cupboard under the sink. He retrieved it, along with spare batteries and candles from a kitchen drawer. He arranged the candles in a semicircle in front of the sofa. Looking upon them once they were lit, they put him in mind of some Druid temple where men and women in pitch-black robes performed blood sacrifices to their gods.

He stepped briefly into the storm to peer out on his vehicle, considering whether to bug out of this situation and head toward town. His car, barely discernible, was now half-buried in snowdrifts. Even if he could dig it out and get it started, he'd still have to maneuver it through several inches of snow on a dark and winding gravel road with limited visibility. No, it was better to wait until daybreak before trying such heroics. That way, if he wound up in a ditch, there was at least a possibility of someone coming along to find him.

Going back inside, it occurred to him that he should let someone know he was stuck on the outskirts of civilization without heat or electricity. The sheriff's office, maybe? Later, perhaps. No sense alarming anyone yet. Better wait until tomorrow and see if it was possible to drive out through this mess on his own.

He'd begun wedging into the sofa and wrapping blankets and coats around himself, when he heard an odd noise coming from the hallway. Probably just another storm noise taunting him. And yet.

Rising wrapped in an Army surplus blanket, one hand clutching the flashlight, he approached the murky corridor.

Cutting through the wailing of the storm rose a distinct and unremitting sound that came from down the hall, from one of the rambler's myriad rooms. He would have described the noise as a mewling, From a cat, perhaps, or some similar-size critter. A raccoon or a hedgehog? An animal of some kind must have gotten in.

He edged open the door to his parents' room and ran the flashlight's beam over the interior.

The room was as he'd left it earlier, but there was something else. Some presence almost tangible but not quite—like a quiver of shimmer just beyond the reach of his perception. No, it wasn't a ghost, but something similar: a spectral presence draped in the cerements of disappointment and lost opportunity. *Loser, loser, loser.* Though unspoken now, he could hear the Old Man's voice ringing in his head and feel the crushing weight of all the Old Man's past judgments and of all his ancillary assessments of who Henry was and who he wasn't. The words tore through him like a pulsing migraine, so severe, it bent his sense of reality

Open-mouthed, he watched as images of his past threaded their way through his present. On his knees, he begged her, "Don't abandon me, Carla. I'll try harder. I promise. Punish me, only don't leave." Staggering on his feet, knuckles scraped, he glimpsed through a haze of intoxication the bloody and unconscious stranger who lay in a heap before him. Fighting back tears, he said, "Listen, Jerry. Couldn't I just stay on part-time? I really need this job." "You've robbed me of everything I've ever wanted to be," the Old Man said, like a judge pronouncing an order of execution. "And for what? So you could squander your existence? You owe me an unlived life."

He faltered backward toward the door, his empty hand grappling for the knob behind him.

Something dropped on his shoulder, and he screamed, but when he tried to brush it away, there was nothing there. Grabbing the knob, he twisted it and threw open the door, just in time to see a ball of fire whiz past from somewhere down the hallway. In a thundering roar, the flaming projectile exploded in the living room, rocking the lakehouse and illuminating the corridor for an instant.

Henry tumbled through the threshold, yanking the door shut behind him. In a daze, he turned the flashlight toward the living room to assess the damage done by the exploding orb, but there was none.

He tottered out for a closer inspection, the light unsteady in his shaking hands. He panned the living room from side to side, from ceiling to walls. Nothing. No sign of a fiery explosion anywhere. Just the room as he had left it, dimly lit by the half-circle of candles.

I must be losing my mind.

Stepping over the tapers, he plopped down on the old sofa's cushioned upholstery, clutching the flashlight to his chest as if it were a lifeline. Despite the cold, sweat beaded at his temples and dampened the skin beneath his clothing. For several minutes, he shook uncontrollably. He pulled over him the blankets and jackets he'd gathered earlier, but they offered no reprieve from the shaking.

What was that ball of fire all about? Had he simply hallucinated it?

His thoughts turned to the revelations he'd witnessed in the master bedroom. If only he could make sense of them. But there was no explanation for these, either. Except, maybe: it was as if the snowstorm had riled not only bears and owls and a crazy old man, but happenings from the frozen soil of his past.

Should he stay, or should he go? But go where?

He stood and, carrying several of the wrappings over his shoulders, he shuffled to the front door and stuck out his head.

Winter now thoroughly iced all the outdoors in its terrible fury. He tried to see through the onslaught to where he'd parked his car but he no longer could. The snowfall was too thick, and the accompanying winds kept the barrage in constant motion. The torrent whipped at his face, and his squinting eyelids began to freeze. Then, from somewhere in the tumult came the angry crack of a tree branch snapping free.

Attempting to flee in this tempest would be madness.

He returned to the living room and tried to think things through, pacing back and forth in front of the candles and the sofa. Was he going through some emotional breakdown? Hallucinating misty poltergeists in the dead of night in his childhood home?

As he sifted through these thoughts, the sound he'd heard earlier resumed: the mewling of an infant or perhaps a kitten, drifting to him from the darkened hallway.

The chill wormed deeper, glazing the marrow of his bones.

Still shaking, he scooped up the flashlight and, moving slowly on numb legs, pivoted back to the corridor. He shined the unsteady beam of the flashlight across the many doors. The mewling was still coming from behind one of them.

It now seemed more urgent than ever that he locate its source.

Fighting through his dread, he took a measured step forward.

As he passed through the sullen hallway, he paused to hold his ear to each door and listened intently. He was nearly a third of the way down the corridor, when he thought he heard something stir in the utility room. Cautiously, he turned the knob and stepped into the dark chamber, sweeping the flashlight's gleam over the washer and drier, the furnace, hot-water heater, and the rest.

Just being in this room made him queasy. This had been, after all, his boyhood penalty box. Or, rather, it had become so after his mother's burial, when it was just Henry and the Old Man in what quickly became the cramped enclosure of the rambling rambler, where the father and son steeped in their mutual resentment. During those toxic days, he'd spent many an hour in the utility room, atoning for misdeeds, real and imagined.

He shined the flashlight on the stool where he'd sat during those miserable hours. He remembered how his tailbone would start to ache, and his back commenced throbbing, and, worst of all, how the relentless boredom slowly ate its way through the spongy tissue of his brain.

Well, whatever noise had alerted him to the utility room had now gone silent, and the odd mewling certainly wasn't coming from here.

He turned to leave when the door slammed shut, startling him. The flashlight fell from his hand, smashed to the cement floor and winked out, leaving the room in total blackness.

As he tried feeling his way toward the door, he whacked his head hard on a furnace duct, nearly knocking himself out. In fighting to maintain his footing, he became completely disoriented, and a deeper darkness rolled in on him from all directions. He became unmoored, floating and bobbing in boundless black.

He'd never felt so alone. So abandoned.

"Why is this happening to me?" he shouted.

But no answer came; only his own words returning to him: echoes from a shoreless void.

He flowed in lonely blackness, in isolation so stark, he felt as if he was the only living being in all existence.

Then, at the edge of infinity, a figure approached. As she grew closer, he recognized her. She was just as he had always imagined her: the Angel of Death. Clad all in ebony with enormous feathered wings, her skull head helmeted, one hand beckoning, the other clasping a gleaming scythe, she'd come to reap him. He knew it was the way of all flesh, perhaps the only way out of this vast loneliness, but as she reached out to touch him, he managed to pull back.

He coiled and squirmed, and soon felt a weight against his chest and legs. He realized he had left the void and was now crawling on the floor, crawling down the hallway, his fingers digging into the flattened gray carpet, dragging himself forward, the wound from where his head had struck the heating duct dripping blood down the sides of his face and from his chin.

At last, he came to the source of the mewling. On the floor, he heard it quite clearly coming from beneath a door. Faint light also came from under this door, but all he could see inside was an expanse of linoleum.

When he stood, he felt like a baby zebra negotiating his legs for the first time. Using the doorknob to steady himself, he rose to his feet, wavering before the entrance he now recognized as that of his mother's hobby room, which his mother had always kept locked. *Son of a bitch, I'll have to break the door down.* But who was he fooling? Dripping a steady rill of blood onto the carpet and wobbling precariously, he barely had the strength to stand.

He was about to try crashing his shoulder into the wood, when he realized the door was no longer locked. He simply turned the knob and entered.

INSIDE, THE WINDOWLESS room should have been too dark to make out details in, but the chamber had its own unique source of illumination: pinpricks of light that hung in the air motionless. These specks—whatever they were—afforded Henry a decent view of the chamber to which he had long been denied access.

It was not at all what he had expected.

Where he anticipated finding sewing patterns and knitting supplies and bound pages of scrapbooked photos, he instead detected nothing more than a room, maybe twenty by twenty, completely empty save for a lone piece of furniture, carefully centered.

The mewling that had attracted his attention now settled into a sort of contented cooing. The noise came from the single piece of furniture: a modest, four-drawer dresser, maple by the look of it, with white-bronze pulls and square, tapered legs. It stood about five feet tall and, aside from the dust that had collected on its top, appeared almost new.

Henry, lightheaded from the loss of blood, teetered forward, feeling as though he were walking through knee-deep gelatin. Or maybe through the detritus of his shattered drive, deflected purpose, and repeated failures. He grinned at this thought: a big, toothy, melancholy grin.

The pinpricks of light were unmoving, yet, at the same time, somehow lacked the consistency of a fixed placement. When he stepped through them, it was like stepping through mirrored reflections, through a dreamy representation of what light specks should look like, if they ever decided to hang in the air, lighting a darkened hobby room in a rambling rambler in the Northwoods of Puposky, Minnesota.

Steadying himself with one bloody hand on the dusty dresser, he slid open the top drawer, making a mess of the drawer's front panel.

No cooing in here, just stacked and neatly folded sleepwear: jammies and onesies and tiny booties. Baby apparel, seemingly never worn.

He closed this drawer and opened the next one down.

101

Here, fluffy blankets in soft pastels shared space with a plush teddy bear, and a long-eared, button-eyed bunny rabbit in an orange felt vest.

Another wave of dizziness swept him as he bent to the third drawer. Blood still fell in a steady drip-drip-drip from his chin and, in this leaned-over position, from his nose. He took a minute to collect himself before pulling out the drawer.

Here were the lotions and salves designed for infants: baby powder, shampoo, oils, diaper-rash ointment. Mixed in with these were plastic blocks, oversized toy keys on a ring, spoons, and a silky-bristled brush.

Nearly doubled over, he wiped the blood from his nose and chin, reached for the bottom-drawer's knobs, and pulled.

The cooing went silent and a heady stench rocked him back on his feet.

Wrapped in a pink bundle lay the desiccated corpse of a tiny, half-formed infant. Hollowed-out eyes stared up at him from a paper-thin skull. On the blanket that swaddled this sad parcel was embroidered an S. For Stella.

He jerked backwards, felt his legs giving out, but couldn't take his eyes from the corpse of his fetal sister, eternally at rest in the bottom drawer of that dresser. He crashed to the floor, tears welling in his eyes, stomach retching. Stella. Why had his parents kept her this way, in a locked room which only they could access? How often had they entered, and what had they done when the hobby room's door closed behind them? Had they spoken to her, sobbing over her lifeless cadaver? Had they cradled her bones to their bosoms, and cursed the day she'd died and the god who let it happen?

He tried to stand, but was too weak. Blood from his head greased the floor and the front of the dresser, and his clothing, and continued in a thin but steady flow down the sides of his face. He would have to crawl out. Get to the phone. Call an ambulance. At least try.

But, for several moments, the horror of the situation gripped him, and he was unable to move.

The pinpricks of light brightened in intensity. From the bottom drawer lifted fussy whines of distress. Not full-throated wailing but the precursor to such a fit. He could hear the bundle shifting within the wooden drawer, though he couldn't see it from his angle on the floor.

Shhhhhh.

The sort of calming noise a nurturer might make to pacify an infant.

A form took shape in the shadows beside the open drawer. No, two forms took shape, and now they both made the calming noise: shhhhhhhhhhhhhh.

Shhhhhh.

Henry's palms slipped in blood as he pushed back toward the open door. He rolled onto his stomach, reached out his shaking hands, found some purchase on the door jamb, and dragged himself into the hall. Behind him, he heard the sounds of a small burden being raised from the drawer, and the shushing noise became purrings of delight. He didn't want to see what was going on back there as he grappled forward, down the carpeted corridor, past the utility room and the master bedroom toward the living room. He viewed his progress through squinting eyes, wishing he could squeeze shut his ears to save him from the delirious goo-goo-gooing sounds that now trailed off into the distance.

The telephone rested in the arc of candles, beside the half-drained cup of coffee. He almost set fire to himself, stretching for the device.

But when he picked up the telephone and lifted it to his ear, the line was dead. Of course, it was.

He again tried standing but it was no use. With each drop of blood, his strength sapped a bit more, and he found himself struggling just to remain conscious.

Then there came movement in the hallway, a shuffling approach.

Terror spurred him onward, across the living room floor to the outer threshold where the wind cried through trees. Somehow, he managed to open the door before whatever it was that shambled from the corridor could reach him. Out he crawled, through the snow and the cold, unable to see where he was going.

Finally, he rolled onto his back, lay in the icy chill, and let the great Halloween Blizzard of '91 slowly cover him in frosty white. As he slipped from consciousness for the final time, he glimpsed his dark angel with her black, feathery wings and reaper's scythe, come to take him away from the misery that even the deaths of his parents had failed to do.

Come to free him, at last.

Call Me Eve

"This world's a city full of straying streets,
And death's the market-place where each one meets."
—William Shakespeare and John Fletcher, "The Two Noble
Kinsmen"

Never mind where I'm from or what my real name is. These things haven't been spoken of in so long that sometimes I forget them myself. Let's just say I come from a time before the universe anointed its latest gods and, as far as my name goes, call me Eve.

First of all, trust me when I say what you believe to be reality is a second-rate imitation at best, its rules of order being too rigid for anything other than a lower life form to populate. Gravity, energy, refraction, laws of motion, thermodynamics, it's all just alphabet soup. Meaningless narratives told to keep the simpleminded from tearing out their hair and leaping from bridges. The genuine nature of reality is beyond anything you could imagine and infinitely more frightening.

What would you say if I told you supernatural forces are what ultimately govern your life? That from time to time, you dance on strings operated by the spectral hands of demons and invisible predators?

You know that secret of yours? The one you would never tell anyone, even on threat of death? Why do you suppose you acted that way, said those things, or otherwise chose as you did? You say it was a moment of weakness?

Don't make me laugh.

Your entire life is composed of moments of weakness. You grovel for your pay, plead for understanding, prostitute yourself for affection, and relinquish what little power you possess to those who could clearly care less about you or your problems.

But I digress.

At bottom, all of your lives are the same: a variable number of years lived in a succession of seasons, marked by spectators who tolerate you to a greater or lesser degree than you imagine. Occasionally, you may achieve some small accomplishment, possibly even some deed noteworthy enough to record in cyberspace, where it eventually becomes buried by the unending flotsam of others' mediocre achievements.

Nothing in your life has lasting meaning. A generation or two after your death, no one will even remember you.

Yes, there are rare exceptions, but you are not one of them.

Over eons, I've watched your Earth grow colder, more brittle. Your greatest art is now that which is born from suffering. Your towering steel-and-glass edifices are built on the broken backs of the destitute. Your countries weal hideous weapons of war against one another's children without blinking an eye. You foul the sky and the waters with your filth. And wonder what you have done to invite the meddling in your lives of dark entities from beyond.

Well, wonder no more.

In all fairness, though, it's more or less as it has always been.

It always ends with you, your voice quavering with fear as you beseech me to spare you another day. Furrows of distress etching your face, spittle dripping from your pallid lips, your pathetic bulk shivering, your bowels threatening to explode.

Well, dread not. For now, at least, you will have your wish. For now.

Perhaps tomorrow I will return and take my due. Or the day after. Or maybe a week from now. But I'll be back.

Until then, I'll content myself reaching out to pluck the marionette wires that will deal your life yet another savage blow. After all, I still must have my fun.

The Visitors

"Gilman decided he had picked up that last conception from what he had read in the Necronomicon about the mindless entity Azathoth, which rules all time and space from a black throne at the center of Chaos."
—H.P. Lovecraft, "The Dreams in the Witch House"

T he Nighthawk canoe, Ramona Jacobs' pride and joy, sliced the gentle waves of Gull Lake as she and her two co-pilots paddled briskly. From over the wooded horizon sailed a bald eagle on the lookout for small game. Nearby, a sleek Northern pike bubbled up, flashing the eagle a tender, greenish-brown flank before diving deep into the dark waters far below. At a distant dock, a bony teenage boy was having trouble boarding a Kawasaki jet ski.

"Probably a city kid," Jodi Higgins said.

"Now, Jodi, be nice," Shayla Shipman said. "Aren't we all city kids now?"

Ramona, always quick to poke fun at the summer tourists who flocked to the sparkling lakes of Brainerd and neighboring fishing villages, replied, "Some of us more than others."

On cue, the scrawny kid, swinging a leg around, upended and splashed headfirst into the drink.

The women laughed.

All three of them, it was true, hailed from bigger towns now, Jodi and Shayla from New Hope, and Ramona from Duluth, but all three were Brainerd-area ex-patriots, graduates of Pillager High School's

109

class of '95. (Husky pride!) In their bones, they were still more country hayseeds than city slickers. And these annual camping trips helped to put them back in touch with their roots.

"You guys getting hungry?" Shayla asked. The biggest of the three women, Shayla, was their canary in the coal mine when it came to food. That is, she could always be counted on to alert the others to the first faint whiff of approaching hunger. She grinned that pleasant, toothsome grin that pinched her cheeks with dimples. "Should we maybe start heading back?"

"Shayla, is food all you ever think about?" Ramona asked, half-annoyed. Ramona was the plainest of the three: a dozen swipes with a hairbrush and the application of the palest lipstick were all the feminine beautifications she had ever mustered. She even cut her own hair, resulting in a sort of boxy pageboy that was her signature look. At Pillager High, she was the tough one: anyone who gave her or her friends a hard time was cruising for a knuckle sandwich.

Jodi stopped paddling, looked out over the splendor of Gull Lake, and said, "I could eat."

The would-be jet skier, sopping wet, had finally settled into the Kawasaki's front seat. He fired the vehicle up in a fog of exhaust smoke, revved the throttle, and took off jerkily at first, then smoother as he got the hang of it.

"I guess the tribe has spoken," Ramona said. "Where do you want to go?"

"Let's grab a burger at Ernie's," Jodi suggested. "That's where we parked, and it gets us in the general direction of the campsite. Then, after we eat, we could get set up before dark."

After they'd put away three Impossible Burgers at Ernie on Gull's lakeside patio bar, the women hauled the Nighthawk Pegasus to Ramona's Jeep Wrangler, where they fastened it in the pull-behind trailer. Then they headed off south on Squaw Point Road.

In the passenger seat, Jodi, sneaking a look at herself in the Jeep's sideview mirror, ran a hand through her auburn hair and admired her mirrored aviator sunglasses. She still had some of that schoolgirl freshness to her, but she realized it wouldn't last long. Soon the crow's feet and the crimps and creases of middle age would creep in to spoil the show. More and more, she caught herself thinking about getting married, having kids, that whole scene, but even if she found the right man, the notion of settling down gave her the willies.

Of the three, Shayla was the only one married.

"How're Darrin and the twins doing these days?" Ramona asked as she maneuvered the Wrangler from the main road to a side one and onto another side one.

"Kids are fine, husband's fine; no complaints," Shayla said. "The twins are walking around and are off momma's feedbags, at last."

"Darrin, too?"

They laughed.

"Well, Darrin's a different story. You know men: they never lose their fascination with boobs."

They laughed again.

It took them about fifteen minutes of driving to get to the spot where they'd first broke camp as teenagers almost ten years ago. This was their place: an isolated clearing amid the Norway pines and paper birch, wide enough to run around in, narrow enough to occasionally spot a deer or a red fox peeping at them from the surrounding treeline. A firepit of char and ash rested off center in the field, and it was to this area they began hauling their gear after first unhooking the trailer from the Jeep.

It took them maybe an hour to get set up. Ramona's Core polyester tent was supposedly big enough to sleep six, but, at eleven feet wide and nine feet tall, realistically accommodated just the three women as snugly as was comfortable. Inside, they brought flashlights, sleeping bags, blankets, pillows, a Coleman lantern, changes of clothes, their favorite board games, several bottles of wine, and enough snacks to satisfy their late-night munchies without leaving a lot of leftovers lying around (which could attract critters). Ramona also brought along a Browning twelve-gauge shotgun in case of a bear attack, though bears had never bothered them before.

Once they settled in, they poured themselves paper cups of Madeira, tossed around a Frisbee, and chatted, Shayla mostly about her husband and kids, Ramona about her job at the Duluth post office, and

Jodi about her parents, who were having health issues and were likely headed for a nursing home.

"It's up to them, of course, if they want to go into assisted living," Jodi said, "but I'd sure rest a lot easier."

As the late afternoon wore on, they gathered wood for the fire, got a blaze going, then cooked up some Field Roast hot dogs and opened a second, then a third bottle of fortified wine. Evening slowly crept in. At the first hint of darkness, the country sky lit up with stars like LED lights on a field of velvet black. A three-quarters summer moon shined brightly.

Ramona rolled a joint, and they passed it around. Between the wine and the smoke, they were feeling no pain.

Their conversation drifted to remembrances of a high-school German teacher named Mr. Faust, who seemed to have too many teeth in his mouth and always wore the same brown houndstooth suit to class each day. His collar and tie hung loosely around his neck, and his shirt cuffs were beginning to fray. When he spoke, it was to the chalkboard, not the students, and he would only turn around occasionally to see if there were any questions, which there never were. The best things about Mr. Faust were that he wasn't much on classroom discipline and always passed everyone, whether they'd understood any German or not.

Ramona was about to introduce their gym teacher, Miss Peters, into the conversation when Jodi pointed to the heavens and said, "What do you suppose that is?"

Jodi's finger indicated an object in the evening sky: a glowing, ruby-red disk, surrounded by a red outer ring, that glided through space in a manner reminiscent of a Roomba vacuum cleaner. Judging distance was tough, but it looked to be flying pretty far up, maybe as far away as a commercial jet would fly. Maybe a little closer. The wine and the dope toyed with their sense of perspective, making it harder to gauge. The object's sparkle had a rainbow luster to it.

"Ramona, where'd you get that weed from?" Shayla asked.

The three laughed, if uneasily.

"Is that a UFO?" Shayla asked.

"Don't have a cow, Shayla," Ramona said. "It's probably a just a drone tricked out to look like a flying saucer to freak out the locals."

"Yeah, that's it," Shayla agreed. But she pinched out the blunt's coal, just the same, figuring they'd had enough smoke for now.

They followed the disk with their eyes as it made its way across the ether. It paused, hovered, then dipped as if scouting a place to land. A blinding white spotlight came alive from the object's metallic underbelly and shined into the trees not far from where the women sat.

"Must be a big drone, though," Ramona said.

"Must be a hell of a big drone," Jodi said.

As the device drifted lower, it kept getting bigger and bigger until its true dimensions appeared to be about half the size of a football stadium. Portals appeared in its ruby rim. It hummed, but barely audibly.

"Holy shit," Ramona said, as the three watched slack-jawed. "Quick. Someone take a picture."

Shayla fumbled her smartphone from her jeans pocket. Her carrier showed no reception bars in this part of the country, but the camera would still work. She clicked off a few shots.

The spacecraft—there could no longer be any doubt that it *was,* indeed, a spacecraft—settled among the trees. Its crimson light winked out, and for several minutes, neither it nor the women made a sound.

Looking lost, Shayla finally broke the silence. "What do we do now?"

"Let's get a closer look," Ramona said.

"Or we could climb in the Jeep and start putting some miles between us and that *thing*," Jodi offered.

"Hang on," Ramona said. "We don't really know what we're dealing with. It could be some kind of clandestine government warship, or it could be a genuine flying saucer with real-life aliens. Do you want to spend the rest of your life not knowing?"

Jodi looked unconvinced. "What if it hurts us, Ramona?"

Ramona eyed Shayla. "You want to weigh in on this?"

"I don't know what to say."

"Listen," Ramona said. "How about if I go in for a closer look? You two wait here, and I'll sneak a quick peek."

She started moving across the clearing toward the dark treeline of Norway pines and birch.

"Wait." Shayla said. "I'm going with you."

Jodi's will waffled. "Me, too, I guess."

IT WASN'T THE BRIGHTEST OF NIGHTS, but it gave off enough auxiliary light for the three of them to see well enough to stagger through the trees and brush of the forest toward the spot where they judged the spacecraft came down. They'd walked about ten minutes when the soft hum of the vehicle started up again and, silhouetted through the tree branches, the clearing before them lit up in glaring red. They emerged in the open field just in time to see the saucer disappear into the night sky, leaving behind an empty clearing, devoid of even a crop circle.

Ramona kept saying "Holy shit," as if it were a religious incantation.

They kicked around in the clearing for a while, assembling their thoughts.

Then, Jodi said, "Now what?"

"Looks like our excitement is over for the evening," Ramona said. "Let's head back to camp."

They tottered back in silence, an occasional tick or snap reminding them that the forest at night has denizens of its own: nocturnal hunters prowling for lesser game, cunning eyes shining in the shadows. Here, human beings were the intruders.

They gathered around the campfire, tossed in a few more branches, sat staring into the flames. "Good thing we got pictures," Jodi said, "or no one would believe us."

The other two grumbled their assent.

"Do you think that really was an alien spaceship?" Jodi asked.

"Sure," Ramona replied, propped back on her elbows. "A flying saucer full of cuddly little creatures that look like Chewbacca," she said sarcastically. She leaned forward and relit the joint from a flaming stick and puffed. "Who knows?" she asked, passing the smoldering herb to Shayla. "Let's just say it was, and that they were friendly little buggers and leave it at that."

Their heads were spinning from excitement fused with intoxicants.

They scoured the night sky for a glimpse of ruby red but found none.

"I'm going to pee," Jodi announced at some point, standing up unsteadily. "Anyone need anything while I'm up?"

"More Madeira," Ramona said, then she and Shayla picked it up as a stoner chant: "More Madeira! More Madeira!"

"Okay, you two," Jodi said, moving toward the spot of dense forest that was their official peeing place.

Stepping deep into the gloom, Jodi was about to squat when—

She froze. Something was in the woods with her. She turned a half-circle.

What stepped into the blades of moonlight and met her gaze was no kindly, comic-book caricature with twinkling, almond-shaped eyes and a winsome tilt of the head. Instead, the figure before her loomed eight-feet tall, and had long, thickly muscled arms dangling from hunched shoulders, long legs flexed as if ready to spring, and multi-jointed fingers curling slowly into fists. All it wore was a sort of sleeveless smock that draped its torso to the knees, and an empty sling that hung from one shoulder.

The structure of the creature's head resembled a narrow, tear-shaped Christmas light, rounded at the top and pulled down to a dull point at the chin. The face was pasty-gray, with black eyes, a tiny, black slit of a mouth, and a hard, black, beak-like nose that softly bubbled and squeaked as the creature breathed. The skin over its skull rested loose and masklike.

Jodi took a slow step back.

At the campfire, Shayla and Ramona, unaware of the strange visitor's proximity, murmured and giggled into the night air. Shayla said, barely audibly, "It's nice to get away from all that drama in the city, don't you think? The shootings, the carjackings. Out here, all we have to worry about are bears and alien invaders."

Ramona said something unintelligible, and the two women laughed.

Jodi took another step back, holding up her hands in what she hoped was a reassuring gesture. She tried to say something, tried to cry for help, tried to scream, but all sound caught in her throat.

Now the face that loosely draped the creature's head came closer. The multiple-jointed fingers stretched wide as the open hands approached, lightly touching either side of Jodi's head, then twisting it with a savage resolve and yanking it free from her neck. Auburn hair draped the fresh face of the dripping skull as the rest of the body collapsed into the shadows.

The creature looked into Jodi's sightless eyes for a minute before depositing her head in the sling at its side. One down and two to go, the creature seemed to reason as it fell to feeding on Jodi's lifeless corpse.

"JODI!" RAMONA CALLED. "Did you get lost in there or what?"

"Where's our wine?" Shayla added drunkenly. They took up their chant anew: "More Madeira! More Madeira!"

"I don't think she can hear us," Ramona said. "Let's give her a few more minutes."

Shayla took out her smartphone and scrolled through the pictures she'd taken. "Here's a good one," she said, handing the phone to Ramona. They gave it back and forth, remarking on the various photos. At one point, Ramona, high as a kite, nearly dropped the phone into the campfire.

Another ten minutes passed, and the women grew antsy.

"We should check on her," Ramona said, slurring her words.

They stood, brushing dirt from their seats. Shayla took a clumsy step toward the woods, when Ramona stopped her. "Let's get the shotgun," Ramona said, suddenly serious. "Just in case." She ducked into the tent and came out holding the Browning twelve-gauge and a flashlight.

She tossed the flashlight to Shayla, who bobbled it.

Then Ramona cracked open the shotgun, loaded in two shells, and ticktocked it shut. "Let's see what's up," she said.

"Jodi!" Shayla called. "Did you fall asleep in there, or what?"

Still no response.

116

Shayla again: "Jodi? You in there, hon?"

They stepped through the trees, into the motionless dark, and the flashlight's cold beam fell upon what remained of their friend.

Shayla shrieked. Ramona's knees trembled.

In a pond of black blood lay a headless corpse, a bloody spinal column jutting from the neck region. Something had crushed and ripped open the torso, flailed at the insides, and torn away chunks of organs and intestines. Splintered bones poked through fabric and flattened remnants of flesh. Part of one leg was gone. Their fresh-faced friend had been reduced to an ugly spectacle of gore so hideous that their minds rebelled against the very sight of it.

They stumbled into the clearing as if jolted backwards by a surge of electricity.

Ramona's legs buckled, and she and the heavy shotgun fell to the ground. Shayla collapsed to her knees and lost her lunch. They both shivered uncontrollably.

Ramona was the first to regain some passing semblance of clarity, though intoxication and lightheadedness were ganging up on her. She reached out for Shayla's shoulder, shook it, and said, "Come on. We gotta get out of here."

The dazed expression on Shayla's face told Ramona, even in her stunned condition, that shock was setting in.

"Come *on*." She picked up the Browning, then, grabbing her by the elbow, she helped Shayla to her feet and led her across the clearing toward the Wrangler. "Move, Shayla, *move*," Ramona prodded.

Now the summer night sounds of cracking twigs and rustling bush took on a more ominous tone. Whatever had done those terrible things to Jodi was still out there somewhere.

Tipping at the verge of unconsciousness, Ramona all but dragged Shayla to the Jeep's passenger seat, set her down, and buckled her in.

She had a moment's terror on not finding her keys in the first pocket she plumbed, but the fear abated when she touched the metal ring in the second. Her hand shaking, she engaged the ignition, threw the Wrangler into reverse, maneuvered around the canoe trailer, and peeled out backward. Now, out on a connecting road, they rocketed forward, rear tires streaming side to side. Ahead lay a sharp curve, manageable at twenty miles an hour, but perilous at fifty. Ramona slid into the turn, felt the steering wheel jerk in her hands, and the next thing she knew they were airborne.

The resulting crash was fierce enough to lift the Jeep's rear tires from the ground.

"RAMONA, WAKE UP! Wake up, goddammit!" Shayla's voice called to her through foggy grayness.

Something jostled her, and the movement flooded her side with excruciating pain. It felt as if she'd been knifed with a bayonet. "Ow, ow, ow," was all Ramona could say.

The Wrangler's headlights shined on the trunk of a Norway pine that looked barely dented. The front of the Jeep, though, that was a different story. The collision had folded in the front fender, buckled the engine hood, and ruptured the radiator, creating a mist of sizzling water vapor.

For her part, Ramona had been thrown from the driver's seat and squeezed into the windshield. When she'd thoughtfully buckled in Shayla, she'd neglected to do the same for herself. Her forehead and nose were bleeding, and an incisor hung loosely in her mouth. She pulled herself from the glass and sat back in the driver's seat.

"I think I broke a rib," she said.

Shayla, her face looming wide-eyed and bloodless, said, "We g-gotta get out of here."

Three shades of woozy from the crash, the weed, the wine, the memory of the spaceship, and the sight of her friend left in a headless mess in the dark of the woods, Ramona said to the ghostlike apparition that was Shayla, "Where's the shotgun?"

Shayla looked around, panicked. "Must be in the back. Where'd you leave it?"

Ramona reached behind the seat and felt around. The action brought a piercing pain to her side that emptied her lungs and had her seeing stars for a minute, but her hand clasped the metal barrel of the Browning, and she swung it awkwardly into her lap.

That's when the passenger-side door flew open, and a hand composed of fingers with myriad joints stretched forth and effortlessly snapped the seat belt from around Shayla. "Shoot, Ramona, *shoot*," she pleaded.

"But I'll hit you, too."

Before Shayla could say anything more, the hand abruptly whisked her out the door and into the night.

Ramona pawed at the latch of the driver-side door, got it open, stepped out shakily with the shotgun cocked, and laid it across the roof of the Wrangler. She drew a bead and fired. The recoil went straight to her injured side, and, for an instant, all she could see was red.

As her focus returned, she discerned where her shot had nearly cut in half a towering, thickly muscled monster with a loose-skinned, otherworldly face, clad only in a sleeveless smock. From a blood-dripping sling under one arm cascaded auburn hair Ramona recognized at once.

The beast's grip slackened, and Shayla broke free.

Ramona was aiming a second shot when, behind the creature, the bush came alive with movement. Other hunched giants in sleeveless smocks sprang forward, summoned by their comrade's cry, a dozen black eyes glistening in the moonlight, searching out the creature's tormentor.

They all bellowed angrily at Ramona, sounding something like a choir of bull moose calling over a ham radio.

Still gripping the shotgun, Ramona dove into the Jeep. The key was still wedged in the ignition. She twisted it, but got nothing. Then she realized the car was still in drive. She slammed it into park and tried again. This time the battered engine roughly coughed to life, a clanging sound coming from under the crumpled hood.

Shayla was almost in the vehicle when several hands with multi-jointed fingers yanked her back. Her screaming was awful.

One of the creatures started climbing into the Jeep from the passenger side. Ramona took her hands off the steering wheel and seized the shotgun. Its roar in the confines of the Jeep was like a cannon going off.

Ears ringing, side throbbing, bloody-faced, and terrified to the brink of insanity, Ramona cranked the steering wheel, tore through the gears, and blew through the brush, searching for a road. The space

119

monsters that weren't tearing at shrieking Shayla lunged after Ramona, bellowing to one another.

She spun hard left, soft right, then felt the tires bite into gravel. Rocks flew as she fishtailed down the roads, finally separating herself from the pursuing creatures.

The clacking under the hood grew fierce, and her dashboard lit up with warning lights. "Just a little farther," she coaxed, but the Wrangler wasn't having it. The engine seized and died. Repeated attempts to restart it were fruitless.

She grabbed the shotgun, then realized she'd shot her two, and the rest of the shells were back at the campsite in the tent. So, she tossed it aside, opened her door, and ran down the road for all she was worth. Every stride brought knifing pain to her side, but she could still hear the muscled fiends coming behind her, so she ran through it all: the confusion, the shock, the terror, the remnants of the intoxicants swimming through her bloodstream, and, of course, the dagger of anguish in her side. She must have run a country mile, sometimes barely maintaining a hold on consciousness.

Finally, she could run no more. Coming to a huffing stop, sobbing wildly, she bent forward and held onto her knees to keep from falling over. But then she did collapse and she shivered from the feeling of her sweat going cold in the night breeze. She fought to keep her hold on awareness, but it slipped from her.

She felt the clinch of nothingness.

"MISS? ARE YOU ALRIGHT?"

A hand gently nudged her shoulder.

She lay facedown in weeds and grass, and realized someone was bowed over her, talking to her. "Miss?"

She worked a hand under her and rose to an elbow. She blew hair from her face and squinted up at a kindly-looking old man who put her in mind of a farmer. His palm rested on her shoulder.

"Can you get up? Do you need help getting up?"

She pushed herself to a sitting position, her wounded side protesting painfully. She looked around hard in the night for the space monsters, but there was no sign of them. She wondered how long she'd been lying there.

The old guy was, indeed, a farmer, though a retired one. He told her his name was Sumpter. Sumpter Kane. He wore a checkered flannel shirt, OshKosh B'Gosh coveralls, and a straw hat. His eyes were a cloudy blue, and his face was lined and leathery from countless hours in the sun.

He helped her to her feet.

"What time is it?" she asked.

"Close to eleven, I'd say. How'd you wind up here?"

The events of the evening barreled through her mind with the force of a freight train, and she was explaining to him how she had gone from canoeing in Gull Lake to running through the countryside for her life. The story came out disjointed, out of order, and must have sounded like crazy talk to Sumpter, but if it did, he wasn't showing it. He nodded, stroked his chin, took off his hat and fanned himself with it, then put it back on. He listened soberly as she went on about ruby-red flying saucers; extraterrestrial beings with black eyes, black mouths, and black, beak-like noses; about friends being torn apart and flattened; about the galaxy opening a hole in the sky for all its madness to scramble through.

"There, there," he said, putting a grandfatherly arm around her. "Let's get you inside."

"You must think I've lost my mind."

He was silent for a moment, then he said, "I've lived in these parts all my life, and I'd be lying if I said you're the first one to tell me a story like that. They say if you live long enough, you'll hear it all. See it all, too. Nothing surprises me anymore."

He led her toward a farmhouse in the near distance.

"What about a spaceship?" she said excitedly. "Did the others say anything about a UFO?"

He took his time answering, framing his thoughts carefully. "I've seen things that would curl your hair. I gave up trying to tell people about them years ago. They thought I'd lost my marbles, and maybe they were right. You live your life thinking things are a certain way, and when they stop being that way, either you were wrong about how

121

things were, or you were right, and all reason has just failed you. Or maybe both those things are true. Who knows?"

"Does that mean you *have* seen the spaceship? Maybe even the monsters?"

They came to the farmer's driveway and approached the front step. The inside door was open, and light poured through the screened outer door. "I learned long ago to accept the things I cannot change. I didn't choose to have the devil move into my backyard, yet here he is, tunneling beneath the very soil that nourished my family's crops for years and years—building his cities out of sight. That's where the devil likes to play, where you can't see him. If you do meet him, you'd better have an *understanding* with him. Or the devil will have you for lunch."

He held open the screen door for her. "I'm real sorry about this, hon," he said.

She stepped through, and Sumpter closed the door behind her, preferring to stay outside. He sat on the step and looked at the stars.

Inside, fingers with multiple joints clasped her upper arm in a vicelike clamp, and led her to a table where seven of the space creatures sat, their breaths gurgling in their black-beaked noses. They turned the loose skin of their pasty-gray faces toward her and watched as she was guided to the table. Additional creatures rose and helped position her in the center of the table despite her loud and panicked protests.

They held her down, and their black, slit mouths opened as one, as they leaned into her and began to feed.

Beaned

"He shut his eyes, grateful for the faint breeze that seemed to cool his throbbing brain. He experienced a dull sense of unreality. He was a stranger in a strange land, a land that had become suddenly imbued with black horror."
—Robert E. Howard, "Pigeons from Hell"

Bruce Loomis, fifty-four, drifted at the edge of consciousness in the cottony haze of a somnolent realm. He realized at once something wasn't right. Something as fundamental and personal as his given name or his darkest secret. Something at the very core of who he was. But, for the moment, he was content to drift.

When, at last, he tried to flutter open his eyes, intense brightness assailed them. His eyelids quickly squeezed down hard, and brilliant afterimages swam in blackness for several more minutes.

As these images slowly faded, he became aware of sharp and vivid odors he had never smelled before. When he tried to categorize the aromas, the best he could come up with were things like the heat that radiated from a television screen or the starchy scruff of white linens rubbing together or a cart with metal instruments wheeling in a distant hallway. Not the sort of things he would ever have associated with the sense of smell.

He tried opening his eyes again, and this time was somewhat successful. That is, he managed a Clint Eastwood type of squint through which he glimpsed the shadowy outlines of a bed, a cabinet, medical instruments, and a TV screen. Then, one of the medical devices beeped,

123

and he knew this not only because he heard it but also because he tasted it—a caustic, metallic taste at the tip of his tongue.

The shadowy surroundings solidified, but they didn't take shape in the ways he would have expected. Everything seemed out of proportion and had a smoky haze, and the details and the colorings of objects seemed to slip just outside the outlines of their boundaries. The light from overhead trembled in intensity, and when it caught on a glass or aluminum surface, it fractured into sparkly bits.

He closed his eyes and tried to think. *What was the last thing I remember?*

The bite of winter's cold. Snow on the lawns. His two dogs on leashes. The pharmacy across the busy street. *Bass Lake Road*. He had been walking Phoenix and Abu along Bass Lake Road when …

Ice on the sidewalk, a momentary loss of footing, coming down hard.

That was it! He'd slipped on the ice and must have smacked his head and knocked himself out.

Someone else entered the room. This time, he opened his eyes more fully and saw a form he could only interpret as being a nurse. She had on an oversized, old-fashion nurse's cap (which he was reasonably sure no one wore anymore) and a uniform that appeared pixilated. Her nose was enormous, and a black hair of prodigious length sprouted from her chin. A strange, visible energy emanated from her like an aura. He somehow knew her name, Agnes, and she wasn't getting along with her boyfriend.

She stopped midstride and looked at him as if she wasn't sure what she was looking at.

"Mr. Loomis?" she said, her words tasting to Bruce like moldy apple cobbler.

He opened his mouth to acknowledge that he was indeed Mr. Loomis, but all that came out were a wheeze and a grunt.

"Let me get the doctor," she said, hurrying to the door.

Talking now apparently required some skill set that temporarily alluded him. He concentrated, trying to work his words through twisted mazes of meaning and articulation, but by the time he managed a tepid

"Okay," Agnes was already gone, leaving behind an oddly earthen scent.

Other figures moved past the open doorway; each engulfed in an aurora, each with color and characteristics that roved beyond their outlines. Many with disproportionate features and limbs that surpassed the grotesque. Some loped, some slinked, some skipped, some hopped as if in potato sacks, but no one just walked.

By the time the doctor arrived, Bruce had skilled himself sufficiently at speaking to ask, "What happened to me?"

The doctor, an anthropomorphic dummy with unblinking eyes and used-looking skin, replied, "Mr. Loomis, you're at North Memorial Hospital in Robbinsdale. You arrived by ambulance three weeks ago. Do you remember any of this?"

Bruce shook his head.

"You slipped on the sidewalk. Got beaned pretty good." The doctor pointed at the bandages on Bruce's head. "You've been unconscious ever since." As the doctor spoke, his words became symbols that floated from his mouth and collected near the ceiling lights. "How do you feel?"

He wanted to answer "discombobulated" or "inside out." Or maybe "hooked up all wrong," but instead he said, or seemed to say, "A little weird."

As he moved to Bruce's bedside, the doctor stepped out of his white coat, which hung in the air behind him for an instant before once again draping the doctor's frame. He held a penlight in a comically extravagant cartoon hand, shined it in Bruce's eyes, and drew his puzzled face closer. Bruce could see into the doctor's pores at the muscle and bone beneath the skin.

"Do you feel nauseous?" the doctor asked.

Bruce shook his head. The action put all his awareness in blurred motion.

"Dizzy?"

"A little."

Arteries that crawled in the whites of the doctor's unblinking eyes began to writhe. His breath smelled suddenly wormy. "We're going to keep you under observation for twenty-four hours. Run a few more

125

tests. Make sure you're mended sufficiently before sending you home. You took a serious blow to your head." He clicked off his pen light. "Do you have any questions for me?"

Bruce thought for a minute. Then he said, "Where are my dogs?"

TWENTY-FOUR HOURS BECAME FORTY-EIGHT, then seventy-two, then ninety-six, and still the aftereffects of Bruce's fall remained intact. A series of specialists with anime appendages examined him, poked him, moved his joints, and asked him questions. They offered tepid diagnoses but, when pressed, could only scratch their collective jaws in quandary.

The fall had cracked his cranium, caused his brain to swell, and resulted in a tear of his arachnoid membrane and a nasty lesion on his cerebral cortex.

Even as the swelling had subsided, the hallucinations remained.

"I feel like I'm witnessing reality through a kaleidoscope or funhouse mirrors," he told his sister Shelly on one of her frequent visits to the hospital to check on him. "My senses seem all out of synch and overlapping and distorted. It's like I'm stuck in the wickedest acid trip ever."

"How's your mental health?"

Bruce thought for a minute, then said simply, "Confused."

Shelly knew something about mental health. Many years ago, when a childhood friend, Kelishea Taylor, committed suicide, Shelly took a silver jackknife to Uncle Morven. She blamed their uncle for causing Kelishea's mind to have come undone. She was not alone in this belief. Everyone blamed him but proving it was another matter. Shelly, though, had all the proof she needed. Her act of retribution cost her twenty years in the Minnesota Correctional Facility in Shakopee.

Murder generally destroys two lives: the victim's and the perpetrator's, but if Shelly was reduced by taking Uncle Morven's life, she never once showed it. Instead, she took her sentence stoically, served her time without protest, and apologized to no one.

But that bit of nastiness was long ago.

"When are they letting you out of here?" she asked, looking to Bruce more like a Picasso abstract than his chubby, sixty-some-year-old ex-con sister.

"Tomorrow, they're moving me to some rehabilitation outfit called The Residence in St. Louis Park."

"How do you feel about that, Bruce?"

"Well, I'm ready to be out of here but not ready to be on my own, not in my condition. Hopefully, these hallucinations will clear up with time, so maybe it's the best place for me. For now."

"You could stay with me and Lillian. The apartment's small, but there's a back bedroom we're not using for anything." The offer was sincere, he intuited, but his presence would be awkward, infringing on his sister's privacy. Her Picasso eyelashes turned into spiders and crawled off across her head.

"I think I'll give rehab a go," he said.

SHORTLY AFTER CHRISTMAS the doctors released Bruce for rehabilitation. Shelly took the afternoon off work to drive him to The Residence and get him acclimated.

He couldn't walk very well, his equilibrium all but nonexistent. Even being pushed in a wheelchair made him feel like he was falling. He gripped the armrest pads for dear life.

On the ride over, in her cluttered '92 rat trap of a Buick LeSabre, she told him how she and Lillian had put up handbills with a photo of his missing dogs in business windows, on community cork boards and on tree trunks throughout New Hope. A stack of the fliers slid around in the back seat.

"I put my cell phone number on the posters," she said, calmly operating the steering wheel. "So far, the only calls I've gotten are from cranks and perverts. One said he'd be my dog if I gave him a biscuit." She chuckled.

It never occurred to him or to Shelly to check with the old woman on Gettysburg Avenue North who Bruce had bought the dogs from.

Prison tattoos covered Shelly's arms from fingertips to shoulders: a three-bladed ax in a circle of fire, disembodied wings impaled with tridents and arrows, thorny vines entwining a horned crow, and so on.

The sleeves of her winter coat now hid most of the tatts, but a lizard-headed bat holding a lyre on the back of the hand nearest Bruce leered at him. The creature began strumming its instrument, producing faint, sinister chords.

Bruce didn't want to look at it, but it was still better than the view through Shelly's windshield. Outside the LeSabre, Highway 169 unreeled like a 3D horror show. Passing cars piloted by puppets with malformed heads roamed from lane to lane at breakneck speed, sometimes merging into a single car, sometime sideswiping one another. The squeal of tires and crunch of metal created a cacophony that occasionally drowned out what Shelly was saying. Few of the puppet-headed drivers appeared to be paying any attention to the road. One read a newspaper, one applied makeup, one even played a trumpet.

Glass, dislodged bumpers, and shreds of torn plastic and steel littered the asphalt. Every time it rolled over these foreign objects, the Buick jolted and lit up in a blinding flash of light, accompanied by a hard, tinny smell that flared his nostrils, and he would overhear tidbits of conversation, possibly from adjacent vehicles. Or perhaps these were swatches of some sort of intergalactic radio traffic.

It's only a ten-minute trip from Robbinsdale to St. Louis Park, but ten minutes is an eternity when all reality is collapsing around you.

If his senses were to be trusted at all, the LeSabre pulled up at last in a circular driveway in front of an orange-red brick building. The sign out front read THE RESIDENCE, though he doubted the letters were actually lit up in neon.

Shelly went into the building to wrestle him up a wheelchair. When she opened the glass front door, a trapped, decadent smell escaped and, with it, the aroma of dread. A cold sweat came over him. *Am I doing the right thing coming here, putting my fate in the hands of strangers?* But isn't that what most people do every day of their lives to one degree or another?

Shelly emerged from the building, accompanied by a man with wiry, red hair and ears the size of pancakes, pushing a wheelchair. They walked up to the car, and Shelly opened the door.

"How are you doing, Bruce?" the redhead asked through florid red lips, all flappy and rubbery.

Bruce let Shelly and the redhead help him into the chair. "I've been better," he said.

BEANED. THAT'S WHAT BALLPLAYERS CALL IT when they get blasted in the head by a pitcher's fastball. Usually, it happens by accident, when the batter is crowding the strike zone or when the timing of the pitcher's release is off and he loses control of it. Sometimes it's done purposely. When a ball traveling ninety miles an hour goes astray, who can honestly measure intent?

Beaned. It's a funny-sounding word, though the friends and relatives of Ray Chapman, a shortstop for Cleveland, might have taken umbrage at the quaintness of this characterization. In 1920, a fastball unleashed by Yankee pitcher Carl Mays clipped Ray in the noggin and sent him to the hospital for surgery. The shortstop died the next day. Though Ray is the only major-league player known to be killed by a pitch, many others have suffered concussions, required stitches, and had face bones broken. Some developed seizures as a result, some lost sight. The career of Kirby Puckett, whose big bat led the Minnesota Twins to two World Series titles, ended too early when pitcher Dennis Martinez hit him in the face, broke his jaw and damaged his vision. Others also have lost their baseball occupations to an errant pitch.

Beaned. Bruce had learned the hard way that there was nothing funny about getting beaned.

That cold day, when Bruce was walking Phoenix and Abu down the icy sidewalk on Bass Lake Road, he'd been thinking about Uncle Morven, who'd lived in a tiny house on his parents' property in rural Shakopee, not far from the Minnesota River. The chief reason his parents had allowed this reputed child molester to dwell so near them was the disability checks from the government that Uncle Morven shared with them. Money was tight, after all, and every little bit helped. And, of course, he was family, a veteran no less, horribly wounded in Italy during World War Two.

No one knew what he'd said or done to Kelishea Taylor that unhinged her mind that winter night, but everyone knew what Shelly eventually did to Uncle Morven. She'd dropped the bloody knife on the living room floor.

129

When Bruce, awakened by the racket, came out to see what was up, Shelly sat passively on the couch, the blade not far from her feet, staring into the kitchen at nothing, her sleep clothes plastered with Uncle Morven's gore. The front door was wide open, and Mom stood sobbing and shivering on the threshold, looking out on the snowy night.

He remembered his father rushing up to Mom from outside, talking excitedly, holding her. He recalled the shocked look on his father's pale face. The cops came, and then the ambulance, sirens wailed, colored lights flashed ... Shelly led off in handcuffs ... cops had to help the ambulance crew carry out the body bag containing Uncle Morven's massive bulk. Then the days after ... his parents lost and confused ... the newscasters with Shelly's name spewing from their lips. In passing days, Mom and Dad emerging from the dark innards of Uncle Morven's place in plastic gloves with blood-soaked sponges, and bucket after bucket of murky water Dad sloshed out into the snow ... befouled furniture hauled off.

And, there was the way the kids at school looked at him. It seemed as if, after all that, even people who had known him all his life never looked at him the same again.

Beyond the window of his room at The Residence a light January snowfall drifted in from the north. Gusts of wind nudged the evergreen trees that framed the welcoming sign out front. Beyond lay a street lined with abodes that transformed from day to day. Yesterday, they were ominous castles with drawbridges and moats. Before that they were turf houses, fairytale houses, houses formed from gigantic boulders or from driftwood or from piles of bent steel. Sometimes they were skyscrapers, sometimes planetariums. The variety was endless. This afternoon they were two-story geodesic domes, their surfaces glaring like glassy blades in the sunlight.

Elmira, a Nigerian woman with a lopsided, bald head and a profusion of amazingly long teeth, brought in his lunch tray.

"What do those houses look like to you, Elmira?" he asked.

She set down the tray on a bedside table and walked over to the window. "You mean, what color are they?"

"Color, texture, so on."

She thought for a minute. "Well, some of them have brick facings and some are sided in aluminum or wood. They're mostly one-story, and the colors range from tan to sky blue. Is that what you mean?"

"Yes. That's exactly what I mean." He touched together the fingers of his hands. "Thank you, Elmira."

Besides in-room meal delivery and concierge services, the Residence offered an array of therapeutic procedures, though none specifically tailored for Bruce's condition. He tried relaxation exercises, systematic desensitization, rational emotive therapy, vestibular rehabilitation, and neurological physical therapy. Nothing worked. On the medication side of things, doctors prescribed anti-psychotics, anti-depressants, and tranquilizers, in an assortment of strengths and combinations. Some helped a little, and some only magnified the intensity of his visions. Mostly they just made him sleepy or dizzy.

Finally, the therapy stopped, and he quit taking the pills, and the long days of hallucinations and jarring shifts of perception sunk him deep into depression. Now, sometimes he thought of himself in the third person, as if he were outside the cage of his flesh looking in. He mused whether this new world that surrounded him had replaced the real world or merely showed him reality's true nature. Sometimes he wondered if perhaps he was really still unconscious in his bed at North Memorial Hospital and if this wasn't all just a terrible coma dream.

Besides Shelly, he had no other visitors. No wife, no old classmate, no church friend or concerned neighbor. These people did not exist. He'd deliberately organized his life to be that of a solitary figure. Now his sister and paid strangers were the only ones to comfort him in his time of need.

As one season morphed into another, even Shelly's visits became rare, soon limited mostly to special occasions, such as his birthday and Christmas. Who could blame her? He wasn't good company. When he did speak, it was in riddles she couldn't answer or understand. Was all of reality just a puff of smoke? Were our profoundest insights on life just sleight-of-hand trickery and hackneyed platitudes? Was our universe something we could even begin to understand, or was it merely some dark force that trapped us all in its net?

131

Sometimes he let Elmira read to him. Mostly articles from newspapers and entertainment magazines. Teachers threatening to strike; politicians unwilling to compromise; Dow goes up, Dow goes down. Brad Pitt had a new movie coming out. It sounded to Bruce as if he'd heard it all many times before. But he liked listening to the soft Nigerian lilt of her voice.

For her part, Elmira became quite casual in these reading sessions, relaxing in a chair and resting her feet (her "dogs" as she like to call them) on the edge of his bed. Occasionally, she even filed her fingernails as she read. This interaction could have perhaps led to a great friendship, had they both resided on the same dimensional plane.

At first, sleep had offered Bruce something of a respite from the horrors of his day-to-day life. He would lower himself into the black vault of unconsciousness and wrap himself in glorious nothingness. But cracks soon developed in the walls of his ersatz netherworld and glimpses of a new hell emerged from the abyss. All his dreams began to involve being chased. Sometimes he felt the pursuit of an ax-wielding madman, the sound of the swinging ax splitting the air behind him. Sometimes it was a gibbering, odious monster that shook the earth with every approaching step. Sometimes it was a pack of shadowy hounds, barking and howling for his blood.

He would awake mired in sweat and shivering.

He began forcing himself to stay awake to avoid the dreadful chases, sometimes for two or three nights in a row. Nights spent at his window watching gatherings of women-faced owls, or in front of the TV screen as a swarm of white-noise images groped out at him. Alone at night, the hours passed even more slowly than they did during the day, and lack of REM sleep only made his visions more unnerving. Most nights he lay in bed, staring at the ceiling, ghosts glowing in his periphery, listening to dreamers as they spoke to him from beyond the veil. On these nights, he felt a struggle inside him, as if a new personality was splitting off from the old and attempting to gain control of his consciousness.

It was in the stir and grappling of this other temperament that Uncle Morven visited him. Of all the phantasms of his past, he would have thought Uncle Morven the least welcome, but he was wrong.

His uncle's watery eyes had studied him from the shadows. Uncle Morven, vast as a swollen cauldron, draped in one of those once-white T-shirts he'd worn and a pair of torn and tattered jeans that ended at mid-calf, his skin charred red and wrinkled. "Melty man," Shelly had called the old guy when they were kids. He had no ears, no hair, and only a stub of a nose. Triple-chinned, with sunken eyelids hanging crooked and folded, his upper lip pulled back in a perpetual sneer, arms and legs likewise rilled in fiery scarlet, he tested the strength of a visitor's chair beneath the wall-mounted television, drumming the three remaining fingers of one hand on a knee.

"I know you're not real," Bruce said.

The great form shrugged. "I'm real as anything else in this world. As real as the displaced energy of thoughts and motions. As real as the physical embodiment of smell and sound and of heat and cold. As real as the gases, vapors, and miniscule specks of life and death that encircle us in this very room. Can't you feel them crowding the air, Bruce?"

"Did you read that jibber-jabber in a book somewhere?"

"Yes. A book of knowledge and fancy. One of many I've read. And you know what else the book said? It said that these tiny specks of life and death surge, flow, conform, amalgamate, slip through and around one another, and divide into layers. And within their smallest bits lurk whole worlds with teeming, transparent airs of their own. And this wonderment is only the peel on the apple. Don't you see, Bruce? You live in the heart of a miracle."

"And this is supposed to cheer me? Let me tell you something: where I live it feels more like a curse than a miracle."

Uncle Morven chuckled. "We all have our crosses to bear. You think that when they pulled me from that fiery hell in '44, from the banks of the bloody Rapido, and I saw what fate had reduced me to that I wasn't tempted to withdraw into my shell and blaspheme the outer world for its cruelty and unfairness? Of course, I was. But I learned to see beyond my misfortune. I learned to embrace the monstrosity that I had become."

And, just like that, he was gone, leaving Bruce to ponder the meaning of his words.

Why give serious thought to the advice of a delusion? Because it was the first shred of counsel he'd received from *anyone* that rang true.

He'd long ago dismissed the hogwash that the doctors, psychologists, and therapists handed him. And Shelly, gawd love her, when she addressed his condition at all, it was in the form of banal encouragements or vapid optimism. "You'll get better. You'll see."

The truth was that he wasn't getting better and likely never would. These people meant well, but they couldn't see how resilient his hallucinations were; how they'd come to feel as real to him as any other aspect of his life.

Uncle Morven was the first to offer him an example he could sink his teeth into. "I learned to see beyond my misfortune. I learned to embrace the monstrosity that I had become."

Accept the things you cannot change: isn't that what alcoholics said? Lean into the turmoil of your mind, as the Buddhists teach. Live in the present moment.

So what if his present moment was a nightmare of delirium and aberrations? A hundred years from now, he and nearly everyone else on this planet would be dead and gone, and replaced by a whole new cast of characters. What difference will it make then what he decides to do today?

"I learned to embrace the monstrosity that I had become."

That night, when Bruce drifted off to sleep, and the shadowy hounds returned to his heels, instead of running from them, he ran toward them. He seized the pack leader by the animal's shadowy throat and squeezed until the hound whimpered for mercy.

Then he squeezed some more.

THE FOLLOWING DAY, Bruce sat at his window, looking out on houses that were now a strip of slum dwellings. Filth and broken glass were everywhere. One lawn had an abandoned mattress on it. As he watched a rat escape into a sewer grating, he rested in the palm of his newfound equanimity.

This morning he had seen himself in the bathroom mirror for the first time as he truly was: a sea creature, a hydra of sorts, with six snakelike heads, and every head had a triple row of teeth. He found this new Bruce both tantalizingly unsettling and hideously appealing. The bulk of his old personality was now fully tamped down, and the remaining shred had bloomed like a colorful fungus, emancipating a hum of violence that now seethed just below his surface.

He embraced this new self, as Uncle Morven had suggested, and for the first time in countless months felt liberated. Alive.

Elmira brought in his lunch tray, as usual. She paused beside him at his window and chitchatted about the weather.

Bruce reached beneath the cushion of his chair. There rested the metal fingernail file Elmira had inadvertently left behind on one of her visits. He touched its sharp tip with one finger, then he slid it into his clawed hydra hand.

When he finished with this one, he vowed, the pancake-eared redhead would be next.

The Lust of the Hunter

"…Her fingers groping, clawing, the lust of the hunter in her eyes, in her heart."
— Achmed Abdullah, "That Haunting Thing"

Although she wasn't exactly drop-dead gorgeous, she was definitely the hottest woman in the pool hall at 3 o'clock that Thursday afternoon. Possessor of rosebud lips, dewy blue eyes, and flawless, mile-long legs, she wore Daisy Dukes, a summer print blouse, and flip-flops, and had a similarly dressed girlfriend in tow.

She saddled up to the bar, two stools down on my left, chatting up her gal pal as if they were enjoying the most delightful afternoon of their lives. The other guys in the bar couldn't help eyeing the flex of their thirty-something curves.

I, of course, ignored them. That was rule number one: don't let them know you find them attractive.

I nonchalantly read the *Star Tribune* sports pages, making a mental note of the nags racing at Canterbury Downs that evening. Not that I was planning to go there. I sipped my beer.

The ladies made a big production over what drinks to order. When they settled on Sex on the Beach, they giggled like schoolgirls. I caught her glancing at me.

"You girls play the ponies?" I asked, folding my newspaper.

"I lost twenty dollars at Canterbury once. Does that count?" This from the tag-along girlfriend. She had pleasant-enough features and a down-to-Earth quality that was endearing, but was no competition for her leggy chum. She was, at most, a six, while her friend was a solid eight.

"My husband says to bet the number-three horse in every race, and you'll win about thirty percent of the time." This came from the solid eight.

Husband, huh? Was she dangling that out there to see if it would scare me off? Neither of them wore rings except for a toe ring on Tag-Along. Had number eight removed her wedding band for some reason? "That may be the nuttiest system I've ever heard of." Before she could reply, I asked, "How do you girls make a living?"

"I'm a nail technician," said the friend. "Lola lives the life of leisure as a housewife."

"Good for you, Lola," I said, looking deep into her blue-belle eyes. "How do you spend your days? Watching soap operas? It can't be at the racetrack."

She flashed a wide, predatory grin. "Wouldn't you like to know?" She squirmed on the bar stool, which I pretended not to notice.

"My name's Quentin," I said, now looking past her at her friend. "I sell life insurance. I'm going to guess the only life insurance you have is through work."

"Well, yeah. I haven't thought about it much. My name's Bryn, by the way."

She reached across Lola and shook hands with me. She was so trusting I almost felt sorry for her.

"You ladies up for a card trick?" A deck of cards suddenly appeared in my hand.

"Do we have a choice?" Lola asked.

Ignoring her, I shuffled the cards, making sure not to bury the top card, which I knew was a queen of spades. "What I want you to do is count off five cards, like this." As I laid each card down, one after another, I said, "One, two, three, four, five. Then, I want you to look at the top card, memorize it, then shuffle it back into the deck, and I'll pick it out. Got it?"

"Okay," Lola said.

This time, I shuffled the cards so as not to alter the placement of any of the top five. Then I slid the deck toward Lola. She counted out five cards and laid them on the bar.

"Now, don't forget to memorize your card," I said.

Of course, the card she picked up was the queen of spades, which I had placed five cards down when doing my counting bit. It was a simple trick, but the women fell for it. Most people did.

"Know any other tricks?" Lola said.

"Wouldn't you like to know?" I slipped the deck into a pocket.

She frowned.

I smiled. "You have lipstick on your teeth," I said.

The better-looking ones are always taken off guard by a mild dig or backhanded compliment. It's not what they're used to hearing.

For the next five minutes, I focused on Bryn, acting as though I had no interest in Lola. I learned Bryn's favorite pastimes (reading and shooting pool), favorite musical artist (Lady Gaga), and favorite sport (competitive figure skating). I discovered she had a sister in Albuquerque, New Mexico; that she was allergic to bee stings; and that she and her mother had a hot-and-cold relationship that was currently running on the chilly side. She and her father got along well enough, though.

If I asked questions for five more minutes, I'd probably dredge up enough information on Bryn for a biography.

She'd spilled her heart out to me without any reciprocity on my part. Never be too quick to upchuck your own story. To them, I was still what they saw: a sharp-dressed, mustached man with ample confidence, a good listener who knew card tricks. Everything else was what they projected onto me. I remained Quentin, man of mystery.

I turned to Lola and leaned in. I wanted to see if she'd accept me breaching her personal space or if she'd back away. She let me in, relieved I was through ignoring her. I held out an open palm and said, "Give me your hand."

She responded automatically, extending her right hand. I studied it thoroughly, spreading the skin on the creases with my thumbs. "For women, the right hand reveals what you were born with. For instance, this line"—I traced it lightly with a finger—"shows you came into this world with a strong vitality. See how long and deep it is?"

Lola nodded. Now leaning over Lola's shoulder to see, Bryn nodded as well.

"This," I said, indicating a crease that ran from below her index finger to the right, "indicates you show your emotions freely and take control of your own destiny."

Lola half smiled. Her baby blues took on a gleam of fascination.

I finished the reading and turned back to my beer. Lola was still looking at her hand.

"Where'd you learn to read palms?" Bryn asked.

"Here and there," I said.

"Are you psychic or something?"

"Or something."

"Read my other hand," Lola said.

I gave her my sullen face. "You're awfully demanding." I leaned into her personal space and asked Bryn, "She always like this?"

Bryn grinned. "You shoot pool?" she asked.

"I know my way around a table," I said.

We carried our drinks to an unoccupied pool table, Bryn telling me about the hot-air balloon festival held in Albuquerque every year. She and her sister never missed one. "You should check it out sometime. Those colorful balloons bobbing in the clear blue sky, it's magical."

She was already talking to me like we were buds.

Bryn and I played first. She racked, and I broke.

"Don't you want to read my other hand?" Lola said, looking confused.

I was getting inside her head. "The other hand tells your future. You might not want to know your future. Not all futures are sunshine and rainbows. And you already know where it ends. Everyone's life ends the same: one minute, you're as alone as you could be, then the next, you vanish into nothingness."

I broke the unracked balls, knocking in an orange five.

"Looks like you've got stripes," I said to Bryn.

I sank one more before missing a corner shot.

Bryn leaned close to the felt as she lined up a duck on a side pocket, giving me an ample view of her cleavage.

"What about you, princess?" I said to Lola. "Married life treating you alright?"

"Fine," she said, unsure whether to smile or frown. "Marriage has its ups and downs."

"You ever been married, Quentin?" Bryn asked as she tapped in her duck, leaving herself a clean rail shot: ten ball in the far corner.

"I could ask you the same thing."

"Divorced," she said. "Three years. And you?"

"Haven't found the right one, I guess."

"How hard have you been looking?" Bryn's eyes went starry for an instant.

"Not hard enough, apparently."

She rifled the cue ball into the ten, putting enough English on it to leave herself another decent shot.

All this table talk between Bryn and me was getting under Lola's collar. "So, what do you do for fun, Quentin?"

I wanted to say, "Pick up chicks in pool halls," but, on second thought, said vaguely, "All the usual fun stuff." Stay mysterious. Make it tough for them to peg him.

"Have any family?" Lola asked.

"A leech of a brother in San Jose. Don't see him much."

"That it?"

"That's all she wrote."

They kept trying to pin me down: Where was I from originally? What was the name of the company I worked for? Was I religious? Democrat or Republican? On and on, but most of these questions I either deflected or answered half-assed before turning the focus back on the two of them.

By the time six o'clock rolled around, Lola and Bryn had downed three cocktails and were working on a fourth. Bryn had beaten me fairly at the table three out of four times. Lola only beat me once when I intentionally scratched on the eight ball.

Bryn went to the ladies' room, and while she was gone, I moved in on Lola, drawing within inches of her face. "We could have a good time tonight if you're up for it," I said.

Before she could answer, I blew lightly on her neck. Closing her eyes, she curled her face into her shoulder. "What did you have in mind?" she whispered.

I grazed her earlobe with my teeth. "I'm having some friends over for a little party tonight. Maybe you'd like to join us?"

She melted into my arms. "Squeeze me," she said. Then, "Harder. That's it."

She studied me for an instant. "Can I trust you?" she asked.

"I don't know," I replied. "Can you?"

"What about Bryn?"

"She can come along, too. The more, the merrier."

I MUST ADMIT THAT, as we walked across the parking lot, I was quite amazed by the number of dead souls that clung to these two. It was like twin conga lines of the gone.

Bryn especially had an impressive pageant: a stillborn child, a half-wit sister, an incestuous uncle, a crippled playmate, a peasant grandmother from old Russia, and several others. To Lola clung mostly envious women and lustful men in ages from thirteen to fifty. Chances are she didn't remember half these souls. That's the thing about clingers: you don't choose them, they choose you, and it's not so unusual to make a lasting impression on someone you barely remember, if at all.

Most people know at least one person who has died and, rather than pass into the abyss, elected to extend their time on Earth by attaching to a living person. All it takes is your face dawning on them at the instant of death. It's one of many ways to allude the grim harvester, at least temporarily: continue to survive in spirit form by drawing on the life force of one still alive.

I, of course, roamed clinger-free. They knew better than to glom onto someone who carried the beast inside. Some of Lola and Bryn's clingers shivered even now in proximity to me. Tremble on this Earth while you can, parasitic ghouls. Before I'm done with you, you'll wish you'd never passed on the option of eternal nothingness.

The parking lot was well-lit, and I led them to my candy-apple red Tesla Model S. I loved that car. Zero to sixty in two seconds flat, with a top speed of two hundred miles an hour. Space-age interior and a twenty-two-speaker, studio-grade sound system.

Lola stumbled, and I caught her by the elbow. "Sorry, Quentin," she said. "I don't usually get this drunk on four cocktails. My resistance must be slipping."

"No problem, princess," I said. "Why don't we just take my car, and I'll drop you back here after the party?" I now had a hand around each one's waist.

They neither verbally agreed nor disagreed with this suggestion, just piled into the car, Bryn in the back and Lola in the passenger seat. They both looked drowsy. If the alcohol wasn't doing them in, then the sprinkle of powder I'd sneaked into their drinks definitely was.

Either way, there'd be no fussing, no tricky questions to answer, and no last-minute panicking. The cogs were in motion, and from then onward, they'd just keep spinning.

I know what you're thinking: who am I to be acting like God's gift to women?

Look, I'm no George Clooney, but I clean up well enough, and, in my lucky checkered polo shirt and Gucci jeans, I've never had any trouble picking up women. It has more to do with confidence than good looks, anyway. Women will shoot you down whenever they think you're afraid to talk to them. I can't remember the last time this happened to me. If anything, I'd be the one to disengage, if the woman failed to meet *my* standards.

After helping the two with their seatbelts, I climbed into the driver's seat and punched The Pretty Reckless into the stereo system. Taylor Momsen's growling vocals filled the air. I slammed the Tesla into drive and took off.

I had a date with my red mistress, and nothing could stop me. Like Taylor was just saying, the world belonged to me now.

I'VE ALWAYS FOUND IT BEST to move them down the line as quickly as possible. Otherwise, feelings tend to get in the way. You start thinking: aw, she's kind of cute, or sweet, or sexy. You start telling yourself: maybe I should hang onto this one for a while.

But it never pays, especially not on Tithe Moon Night. That is, not on the first full-moon evening of June. That's when the red mistress comes out to be paid. Baba Yaga demands her pound of flesh and woe be to those who disappoint her.

In June of 2002, I remember this guy calling himself Mr. Doom showed up drunk and empty-handed. He had an especially nasty aroma and looked like his hair hadn't been combed in months. For some reason, he only wore one shoe. I remember thinking, how did this guy attract victims? Who in their right mind would let him get anywhere near them?

Mr. Doom came from the Florida panhandle, where most of his wet work focused on male prostitutes, and his crime scenes were notorious for their creative displays of entrails. He said he *intended* to bring an offering but, along the way lost all control of himself. Said the voices in his head kept telling him: do this guy, do this guy, do this guy right here. Said he'd left his intended sacrifice in a roadside ditch outside Clarksville, Tennessee.

This story, of course, held no water with Baba Yaga, who was only interested in sinking her steely teeth into the spécial du jour. Mr. Doom's loss of control, while unfortunate, only made him the target of her wrath.

As you can imagine, it takes a lot to turn my stomach. Blood, gore, eyeballs dangling from empty sockets, those types of things barely register with me. But what Baba Yaga did to Mr. Doom that night, well, that was almost enough to have me scurrying for the puke bucket.

In the light of the moon and the flaming pyres, her scarred hands ripped into his cream-colored flesh, pulling and widening it as if it were composed of carnival taffy. As if it were a latex balloon stretched to the bursting point. Mr. Doom wailed without the benefit of lips. His knees knocked, and he shivered convulsively. His arms flopped uselessly at his sides. He had to turn his head to see through the eyeholes of his own face.

Then the bones of his spine popped and cracked, his hands clutched in jerks and trembles, and he ran with torrents blood and sweat. His pelvis snapped, bringing his thighs together at an unnatural angle. His chest caved in, buckling his entire frame. His shoulders collapsed.

143

His head, now flayed of all flesh, sank heavily into the moist muscles of his neck.

He collapsed. Not sure Mr. Doom was even dead yet, but he was definitely down for the count.

There must have been a dozen of us who witnessed Mr. Doom's undoing at the claws of our red mistress. A dozen shadow skulkers soundlessly watching in awe. Oh, Baba Yaga. You know how to make an impression.

Now barreling north on 371 past Little Falls, the full moon beginning its climb over the pine-topped horizon, Lola stirred in the passenger seat next to me. She mumbled something incoherent, smiled then frowned at me.

Her Temazepam needed a bump.

"Here, drink something." I handed her the water bottle and helped her hold it as she took a deep swig. Her eyes rolled.

"I need to get home," she whispered. "Daniel will wonder what happened to me."

"Relax, princess. We're almost there."

Her eyelids drooped. Her head fell back. A white grain of the powder stuck to one of her rosebud lips.

I glanced into the back seat to see how Bryn was doing. She slept ugly: mouth open, something wedged between her teeth, drool dripping down her chin, her hair mashed to one side. And she snored, though softly. No doubt dreaming of hot-air balloons drifting heavenward in the azure skies over Albuquerque.

OUTSIDE BRAINERD, IN THE TINY HAMLET OF BAXTER, the Arrowwood Lodge offered Tesla Supercharging stations in its parking lot. You could get up to two-hundred miles on a fifteen-minute charge. The women were still sound asleep, so I plugged in, walked to the lodge, and tracked down a bathroom.

The Arrowwood had a luxury, log-cabin feel to it with chandeliers fashioned from deer antlers, and a taxidermized black bear and bull moose glaring down on the lobby from a fenced-in second-floor landing. Behind the counter, a character in a wrinkled bowling shirt and grimy eyeglasses keenly watched me come and go, but didn't say anything.

I was halfway back to the Tesla when I had a hunch that something was wrong. In the moonlit twilight, I saw at once my car doors were open and my passengers missing. *How was that even possible, as drugged as they were?*

144

I caught a flash of white along a far treeline. Maybe it was one of the women's ghostly clingers. Maybe it was just some combination of breeze and foliage and moonbeams. Either way, it was my best hope of catching them before they could spill the beans on me. "Shouldn't be too hard to spot, officer. He's driving a candy-apple red Tesla. Bet you don't see many of those in Baxter, Minnesota."

Off in a full-on run, I headed for the location where I'd seen the flash of white.

I hate to admit it, but middle age robbed me of some zest. Time was, I could have run clear to that treeline without breaking a sweat, but not tonight. Tonight, by the time I got there, I was sopping wet and my breath was burning holes in my lungs. When I'd finally halfway collected myself, I noticed something glowing through a break in the trees. On a narrow footpath sat a flip-flop with a broken thong.

I crept forward.

I couldn't be sure the footwear belonged to one of my quarries, but I liked my odds.

The path wound to the right, and I caught more motion from farther down it. The ghost of Bryn's Slavic grandmother fluttered from sight. Despite still being dizzy and sweaty from my exertions, I charged down that path like Usain Bolt zeroing in on the finish line. Now I could clearly see Bryn limping along on one flip-flop.

Looking back over her shoulder, she saw me.

Her eyes opened wide in terror, and she screamed.

This excited the beast within me, which kept me going.

As I narrowed the gap between Bryn and I, she called out to Lola: "He's here! He's here! Run for your life!"

Tearing through my exhaustion and her spectral conga line of frightened clingers, my hands finally touched the smooth softness of her shoulders, and I spun her around violently.

It was not my face that scowled into hers but that of the beast, and I knew there would be no saving her for Baba Yaga. The thirty-something nail technician who marveled at hot-air balloons in the desert was about to meet a horrible fate. Baba Yaga, be damned. The beast was now in charge, and his only allegiance was to his own lust.

A maelstrom of rage and passion lifted from inside me. The night air shivered with the yowls of Bryn's ghostly clingers.

I remember the sound of ripping cloth, of muffled cries, and slapping flesh; the smell of fear; the taste of anguish; the sudden thick warmth that streamed between my fingers. Before my eyes, she transformed into a twitching thing. A heaving mound of pliable

145

carnality. Her breath already carried the musk of the grave. Her visage morphed into that of a gargoyle.

Then a charge filled the air as her poor spirit joined those of the other dwellers of shallow graves the beast and I had collected over the years. Her clingers wailed and withered as their source of sustenance vanished. The void they had evaded for years reached out and clawed them from this world, and they paid the painful price eventually exacted from most who attempt to cheat mortality.

As the swoon of savagery evaporated, and I could see clearly again, I had to admit the carnage left by the beast was truly impressive, but I had no time to admire it. Lola was getting away and I had to stop her. Try as I might, though, my strength was waning, and the dark forest floor tilted like the deck of a sailboat in rolling waters. Spitting out a toe ring, I dropped to one knee, trying to compose myself.

Then, over the huff-huff-huffing of my ragged breath came the sparkling din of foliage parting. Looking up, I could not believe what I saw.

Not three feet away, an enormous, blue-coated wolf approached and sniffed the air around my head. Somehow, I knew the creature was male. His eyes were a startling contrast: one a brilliant amber, the other a dazzling emerald green. I read his expression as placid curiosity but knew he could turn deadly on a dime. Though wolves seldom attacked people, I wasn't about to test the odds, not with him pulling within inches of my face.

I tried to reach him telepathically to let him know I was not his enemy. But that didn't work. I was afraid that if I spoke, it might spook him.

He tipped his head to one side, studying me.

Finally, I sputtered, "J-just passing through, my brother." I held out my bloody hands, fighting to stay conscious. "I mean you no harm."

He tipped his head to the other side.

Suddenly, I became aware of a new channel of communication opening between us. Only, it wasn't me the wolf conversed with, but the beast I carried within me. They seemed to be getting along fine, though I couldn't understand what they said.

Careful to avoid abrupt movements, I tried rising to my feet, but my legs gave out, and I slammed to the Earth, my cheek splitting on a fallen branch. I lay there, dizzy for an instant, blood pooling in one eye, pulsing in and out of consciousness. I felt like an ant immersed in honey, limbs grappling in sticky sap that just gave, failing to offer me anything tangible to hold onto. All around me, the forest threw shadows. Shadows chased shadows. Something in the wind hammered like a mallet on steel, shooing small birds to flight. The blue wolf's breath, feral and heavy, raked the side of my face, whistled into my ear, and penetrated deep into my skull.

My muscles started contracting. They flexed and relaxed, flexed and relaxed, without any direction from me. The contractions became rhythmic, then violently rhythmic. I was experiencing my first-ever grand mal seizure and was having it in a wooded area in Baxter, Minnesota, within feet of a homicide scene, and in the presence of a wild wolf.

I tried to scream but wasn't able. My bladder attempted to empty itself but I'd already emptied it at the lodge, so I was at least spared that indignity.

Delirium swept me away. I seemed to be running through the forest on four legs at high speed, my face maybe two feet from the ground. Every sinew, every fiber, every neuron in my being focused on the seemingly effortless task of projecting my body forward. My feet barely touched the Earth before leaving it again.

Even though I knew I traveled through a forest at night, my sight displayed a panorama as clear as if I were moving through daylight. Clearer, in fact, as every detail carried a crispness beyond anything I'd ever witnessed before. Between silver shafts of birch trees, I spotted Lola at a distance, her long legs churning in her Daisy Dukes in an unsteady dash. Not only could I see her, but I could also smell her. I could feel the whimpered rush of her breath and the heat of her body, even a hundred yards away.

I felt the panic surge within her as she turned toward the sound of my approach.

Then I blacked out.

How long was I out of it? My sense of time sort of accordioned in on itself. But I awoke feeling confused and tired, my head pounding. Adding to the confusion was the sight of Lola, cross-legged in the dirt, hugging an oak as if it were the only thing holding her to the ground. She stared at me shivering, teeth chattering in her rosebud lips, hair dripping sweat, her pupils the size of nickels.

Why hadn't she run off while I was unconscious?

I also felt a chill sweep my body, but not one of fear. One of ,,, well, chill.

In the cool breeze of the moonlit night, I rested on all fours, *totally naked*. Twigs and stones poked my elbows and knees. I sat up and rubbed my skin, confused.

147

Looking back the way I'd obviously come, I spotted a shred of the checkered polo shirt I'd been wearing.

The soles of my feet protesting painfully, I retraced my path, following strips and tatters of clothing back to the original murder site. My shoes and jeans were the only items spared. They must have slid off of their own accord. I slipped them back on and picked up every bit of my torn clothing I could find. I'm usually much more careful about leaving behind forensic evidence, but under the circumstances, I did the best I could.

When I returned to where I'd left Lola, I was surprised to see her still there, still squeezing the oak trunk, obviously in shock. Then I noticed, towering nearby, heterochromic eyes blazing, my blue-coated friend standing guard, flanks stippled in silvery moonlight. Instinctively, I knew he was on my side, though it took a moment for this to sink in, and I still wasn't sure what to make of it.

My head was pounding, and my cut cheek still bled.

Finally, I said, "Come on, princess, let's go."

Still shivering, she rose.

Back down the trail, through the killing ground, beyond the trees, we walked in the dead of night to my cherry-red Tesla and climbed in— Lola and her ghostly clingers, the wolf, and me.

Looking across at my furry co-pilot in the passenger seat, I said, "Man, this is going to be one hell of a Tithe Moon Night."

Dark Embrace

"Whenever the practical psychology of love becomes a subject of
scientific inquiry — as barren metaphysics now are — and learned
professors are told off to note, lecture, and, if they will, experiment on
its unexplored wonders and universal power, it will come out that
MYSTERY is at the bottom of it all."
—Joseph Sheridan Le Fanu, *A Lost Name*

L anesboro, Minnesota, is about two and a half hours south
of the Twin Cities, just past Rochester on Highway 52. It's a
peaceful if touristy little village of boutiques, galleries, trails,
scenic overlooks, and eateries. The town is renowned for its
thriving community theater, historic bed and breakfasts, and
Coffee Street Walking Bridge, a restored railway span converted to foot
traffic that links Gateway Park to the quaint downtown.

Andaman Greeley, forty-four, balding, chubby, and ruddily
complected, experienced the fading afterglow of a relaxing week's stay
in Lanesboro.

Already, not even halfway home, he sat behind the wheel of his
gunmetal Toyota minivan missing his solitary strolls along the Root
River, his brief, pleasant tete-a-tetes with shopkeepers and fellow
vacationers, his down-home meals at local restaurants, and, overall, the
leisurely pace that accompanies a complete lack of responsibility.

Tomorrow it would be back to reality. Back to the griping
customers and pimple-faced stockboys and -girls, the bored, middle-
aged matrons working the cash registers, and the shuffling retirees,
always eager to prove their worth. Back to Harbo's Garden Center in
New Hope, where he supervised the day crew. Harbo's, where he'd
worked for more than twenty years.

Where, in all probability, he'd work twenty more before the eternal chasm, at last, claimed him.

At a little past noon, he pulled into the parking stall of his apartment building at 49th Avenue North. Lugging a suitcase and an overnight bag, he trudged to the front door and swiped his key fob for entry. The door buzzed. He entered, checking his mailbox, which, naturally, overflowed with fliers and envelopes that, by and large, came from vendors who wanted to sell him something he had no intention of buying.

Riding the elevator to the third floor, Andaman lumbered down the hallway, unlocked his door, stepped into a porcelain-white kitchen with matching porcelain-white furnishings, and set his luggage on a narrow, oval tabletop. *Home again, home again, jiggety jig.*

He unzipped his suitcase, searching for the pastry-shop sugar cookies he'd bought this morning before leaving Lanesboro, and instead came upon a paper sack containing two books. Yes, he recalled the bookshop where he made these purchases. What was the name of the place? Something old-fashioned like Ye Olde Book Monger? Whatever the designation, the owner hadn't bothered to print it on the bag.

He pulled up a chair and emptied the bag's contents on the table.

One of the books was a childhood favorite: *The Merry Adventures of Robin Hood* by Howard Pyle. This edition, a little worn at the edges, featured a colorful cover and titled line-art illustrations throughout. "Stout Robin Has a Narrow Escape." "Robin Meets a Fair Lady." "The Mighty Fight Between Little John and the Cook." "Robin Hood Slays Guy of Gisbourne." The pages had that excellent, old-book feel and smell.

He set it aside and turned his attention to the second volume.

Both of these editions he'd picked up from the bookstore, where crept a strange, gaunt salesman with a goiter on his neck.

Andaman had only expected a customary exchange between himself and the salesman, cash for merchandise. A simple transaction people everywhere are familiar with. But, when he'd put *The Merry Adventures of Robin Hood* on the counter and took out his wallet, the salesman pushed another book across the counter toward him.

"What's this?" he asked.

He would never forget the salesman's reply. "It's the book you came for."

Puzzled and suspecting this guy of trying to strongarm him into buying a second book, Andaman started to protest when the shopkeeper said something about having a knack for sensing what a customer truly wants. He shuddered as he recalled the cheerless way the salesman grinned at him. In the end, not even sure what this second book was about, he paid up: a measly three dollars extra.

Now, he picked up the slim mystery book from his kitchen table and a sensation akin to static electricity hummed briefly in his fingertips. Or had he imagined this?

A hard-bound, cloth-covered edition about the size of a mass-produced paperback, the volume had been handled so much that the title was illegible, both on the cover and the spine. When he opened it for the first time, he saw the pages were rough-cut and brown with age. The title page read: *The Secret Teachings of the Hermetic Order of the Golden Dawn.*

He had no idea who or what the Order of the Golden Dawn was. The Lanesboro shopkeeper must have been pulling his leg. Andaman couldn't imagine why anyone would think this book would interest him.

The next page also spelled out the title, this time in larger letters, and contained the notation "By Frater Perdurabo, the Beast 666."

He went numb with cold. He had no idea who Frater Perdurabo was, but every Catholic school kid knew that "666" was the sign of the devil. He laid the book down carefully and stared at it. *Was this book supposed to have been written by Satan himself?*

Though a lapsed Catholic who hadn't been to church at St. Alfonzo's in years, Andaman still felt the tug of the old superstitions. God, the devil, sin, saints, resurrection. They still resonated with him on some primal level.

Back when he'd decided to stop attending services, Andaman's father said, "If you don't go to church, you know you'll go to hell."

And he'd replied, "Well, I'll worry about that when the time comes." But the truth was, secretly, alone in the dead night when the prospect of death seemed more real, he felt a twinge of worry.

Andaman picked up the book again.

A tiny drawing of a bald man frowned up from below the title inscription.

Fighting a vague dread, he turned the page.

The book, limited to a printing of one-hundred copies, contained spells, instructions, and many illustrations. For instance, it gave detailed directions on how to build a mirror-lined altar room for conducting a Black Mass. It outlined rituals for establishing and strengthening esoteric powers, such as influencing the weak-willed and bending fortune your way. It told him how (supposedly) to become invisible for

151

brief periods and how to call up demons to do his bidding. How to get someone to love you. And, of course, there was a section on speaking with the dead.

When he closed the tome, his hands were trembling. If his father was right and skipping church was enough to cast him into the eternal flames, what fate did owning a book like this one suggest?

MONDAY MORNING CAME as Monday mornings always do for working people everywhere: the shriek of the alarm, the dazed stumble to the bathroom, the all-but-untasted breakfast wolfed down with one eye on the clock, the panicky search for car keys. A mime couldn't choreograph a more slapstick scene.

By the time Andaman unlocked the front door at Harbo's Garden Center, a smattering of employees had already gathered in the dusk. He let them in, and they meandered off in various directions. Lights came on, registers were activated, and workers queued at the coffee machine. He noted that the lawnmower display needed straightening and a cleanup was necessary on aisle three, where some lummox had spilled potting soil.

Making his way to the rear of the building and the warehouse area where his office resided, he barely had a chance to enter and take his perch behind his messy, metal desk when he became aware of someone hovering in his threshold.

"Mr. Greeley?"

He frowned, looked up, and was struck at once by a jolt of recognition and surprise. There stood a winsome blonde in her mid-twenties with violet-blue eyes and perky, pink lips, just shy of five-feet tall and smelling like fresh-picked peaches. At first, he thought she was a vision, a hallucination from his past. But there she was, in the flesh. In the supple, womanly flesh.

Realizing that he must look like a fool, staring at her with open mouth, he turned his attention to some papers on his desk, and said, "Yes. Can I help you?" He felt the heat of a blush.

"I'm Rowena Constance," she said calmly. "I start work here today."

He cleared his throat, picked up a pen, and circled some nonsense on a bill of lading before him. Then, self-consciously, he glanced up at Rowena, and attempted to bluff his way through a few pleasantries.

"I see," he said. "You must be filling in for Colleen Grimwood. She's going on maternity leave next week. Are you from this area?" His own voice sounded to him thin and wandering.

152

"A transplant from Sleepy Eye."

"What brings you to New Hope?" he asked, this time a little too gaily.

"I plan to attend night school at Normandale, once I get settled." That would be Normandale Community College in nearby Bloomington. "I'll be studying small-business management."

"Well, welcome aboard, Rowena," he managed awkwardly. "You'll find Colleen at the cash registers. She'll fill you in on your duties."

He was returning his attention to his desktop when he realized Rowena was extending a hand for him to shake. He reached out, and when he touched it, a sparkling flow of energy ran through his hand, up his arm, and encircled his heart. It was a sensation like none other he had ever experienced.

He nodded to her with a goofy smile and watched hypnotically as she stepped out into the warehouse and moved to the swinging doors that led back to the storefront. Then he got up, closed his door, and leaned against it, out of breath.

The resemblance was striking.

He was twelve years old when he first met her. It was summer, and he was mowing neighbors' lawns, trying to earn enough money to buy a slot car track. It was a scorcher of a day, and he hadn't been hydrating properly. All he could think about was how many more lawns he'd have to mow to get the thirty-five-dollar cost of the track. Believing himself invulnerable, as most twelve-year-old boys do, he pushed himself until he collapsed flat on his back in Mrs. Chan's front yard.

As he lay there, overcome by the heat, a stunning, golden-haired beauty passed through a veil of cloud and floated down toward him, dressed in dove white and surrounded by a peony-pink corona. Her features were smooth, almost silken; her eyes a radiant violet blue; her lips a pale shade of rose. All of femininity combined into one gorgeous package, she drifted within an arm's reach of him.

He looked into the unfathomable depths of her violet-blue irises as she said, "Are you alright?"

He blinked, and just like that, she was gone. In her place knelt Mrs. Chan, looking apprehensive. "Young man, are you alright?"

He sat up, and she fetched him a glass of water.

Was his siren just an illusion? Over the years, he debated with himself many times whether or not he had actually seen this blonde goddess. She'd seemed authentic enough during her brief visit, but— real or not—he never mentioned her to anyone.

Then, over time, she revisited him, mostly in his dreams but sometimes in his peripheral vision, where she lingered just out of clear sight. He would be in the middle of some frustrating task, generally work-related, generally involving the stupidity of one of his employees, when the pink glow of her nimbus appeared at his side, and his storming waves of anger calmed to a trickle.

In his dreams, they roamed together through winding night streets, through bright, flowery meadows and alien landscapes, through forests and deserts, inches above the ground, holding hands. Real or not, he'd come to think of her as his closest friend.

As his one true love.

Today, he learned, her name was Rowena Constance, and she now worked under his supervision as a cashier at Harbo's Garden Center.

If *she* wasn't real, what else in his life was a hoax?

THAT EVENING, he couldn't eat, couldn't read, couldn't even muster the concentration to play computer chess on the easiest level. Instead, he stared blankly at the TV screen, as the images morphed from one spectacle to the next without impacting his perception or awareness.

All he could think about was Rowena Constance, his lady love, apparently come to life.

Throughout the day, he'd avoided the cash registers, not wanting to get too near Rowena, afraid he might further embarrass himself. The last thing he needed was the staff circulating rumors about what a letch he was.

But several times, from a distance, he sneaked glimpses of her as she waited on customers under Colleen Grimwood's steadfast oversight. Each time, the chill of recognition seized him at his core. There was no doubt that this young woman was, if not the angel of his visions, then certainly her exact duplicate.

In bed that night, he stared at the ceiling, wondering how to proceed.

As her supervisor, he'd have to have *some* contact with her, just as he did with all his other employees. But the prospect unnerved him. He was totally in love with a woman half his age who, even in his heyday, would have been out of his league. So smitten was he that he barely trusted himself to get out an intelligent sentence in her presence.

And Harbo's had rules about supervisors and their employees fraternizing as if this were even a realistic option. But if his conduct did upset her, she might have a legitimate case with human resources, which could result in him being fired.

He pondered his situation into the wee hours of the night, before slipping off into the land of nod, his problem unresolved.

Of course, she came to him in his sleep. How could she not?

This time, though, she came with newly added details, which made her seem more real than in the past. Now she had a scent like Rowena: the delightful scent of peaches. And a texture to her speech, a subtle Minnesota lilt. And over her white dress, she wore a persimmon-red Harbo's workshirt and a *May I Help You?* badge

He awoke in a cold sweat.

When he arrived to unlock the store, among those workers awaiting entry was Rowena, her beauty lustrous in the early morning gloom.

"Mr. Greeley?"

He steeled himself to be stern and stoic, but his sternness melted away when he looked into her wondrous visage. "Y-yes. Rowena, what is it?"

"I just wanted to say how well my first day went. Colleen is a fabulous mentor, and I so enjoyed chatting with the customers. My work here at Harbo's feels like *a dream come true*."

Had he imagined the significance of this phrase? *A dream come true.*

Before he could unearth a sensible reply, she was swept off into the swarm of coworkers and disappeared from his sight.

All that day, the misery of the lovelorn haunted him. Glumly, he went through the motions of monitoring the store and its staff, distracted by the relentless aching of his heart.

After work, having swung through the Subway sandwich shop to gather a Veggie Delight on whole-wheat bread, he entered the lobby of his apartment building and encountered a young woman moving in who was trying to wedge into the elevator a lavender loveseat. The conveyance was already stuffed full of chairs and plants, and boxes.

As he stepped forward to lend a hand, the woman turned to face him, and, to his horror, she said, "Mr. Greeley?"

It was Rowena Constance, clad only in cut-off jeans and a man's dress shirt with the lower half knotted above her bare midriff. She beamed at him and added, "Looks like we're neighbors."

"SIR, I'M NOT SURE she's going to work out."

Across the jumble of his desktop, Colleen Grimwood, eight months pregnant, hunkered in the doorway like a tethered zeppelin. Her face had the washed-out quality that results from a restless night's sleep, and though she had made an effort to comb her colorless hair, it dangled listlessly. Her Harbo's workshirt looked in need of ironing.

"Who's not working out?"

"Rowena. The new girl."

Self-consciously, he moved papers around on his desk. "What do you mean she's not working out?" He looked up, attempting to affect a stern expression.

"I mean, she isn't picking up things, and she's terribly slow. I must have told her a dozen times how to clear an entry on the cash register, but she still can't do it on her own. And she spends too much time visiting with customers," here she leveled her eyes at him, "*especially* the male customers."

"I see," Andaman said. "Perhaps you could be a little more patient with her. She's only been here for two days."

Colleen gave him an exasperated frown. "My feet are swollen, my back is aching, and this baby is kicking like a Radio City Rockette. So, if I'm a little short on patience, forgive me." This last part was thinly veiled sarcasm, but he was too abashed to take offense.

"Alright," he said. "Tomorrow, I'll get you somebody else. Maybe move one of the stockpeople to cashier. Move Rowena over to stock. But don't say anything to her. I'll handle this."

Satisfied, she turned and waddled off.

That afternoon, he called Rowena away from the cash registers and walked with her down the wide center aisle to the greenhouse annex.

"Is everything okay, Mr. Greeley?"

He cleared his throat. "How are things working out for you at the register?"

"Fine, I think. Some key functions give me trouble, but the customers are friendly, and I enjoy passing the time with them." Then, she suddenly stopped and turned to look him straight in the face. "Has Colleen said something? Am I being fired? I'll try harder, I promise, Mr. Greeley."

He colored under the intensity of her gaze. "Nobody's getting fired, my dear," he said. *Good gawd! Had I really referred to an employee as "my dear?"* He cleared his throat, coughed into one fist, and said, "But I'm not sure the register is the best spot for you, given your customer-handling skills. I'm considering moving you over to stock, which is less demanding, and you'll have more opportunity to talk with people, helping them find things, and so on."

She brightened. "I'll work anywhere, Mr. Greeley. I'm a team player."

"I have no doubt, m——." He caught himself before he said, "my dear" again.

At the greenhouse, Rowena now walked closer to him, Andaman silently basking in the aurora of her presence.

That evening, he reclined in his robe on his white sofa, trying to concentrate on reading one of the books he'd bought at that odd shop in Lanesboro. Robin Hood, having won the archery contest at Nottingham, learned he'd just shot one of the king's deer, a fete that earned him the official title of outlaw. But Andaman was lucky to get through a whole paragraph before his mind drifted back to Rowena. *Honestly, I'm acting like a lovesick schoolboy!* But, try as he might to chase her from his thoughts, it was only a matter of minutes before she returned.

Setting the book down on his pearl-white coffee table, he took to pacing back and forth in his living room. He tried thinking about chess, replaying a Sicilian Defense opening in his mind: e2-e4, c7-c5, d2-d4, d7-d6, g1-f3, c5-d4 ...

A soft knock came at his door. Who could that be? Rarely did anyone knock at his door.

He looked through the peephole and saw, to his amazement, Rowena holding what looked to be a serving plate. He opened the door.

"Y-yes?" he said, trying to steady his voice as his insides liquified to jelly.

"I'm sorry to bother you, Mr. Greeley. I got your room number from your mailbox. I was just wondering if you'd like some of this banana bread I baked. It's too much for me to eat, and my roommate is cutting back on sweets."

She held out a platter with three fat slices of the fragrant delicacy.

Now her peach scent mingled with the aroma of the banana bread, and pudgy Andaman Greeley in his flannel robe (and in full view of the stunning woman who owned his heart) fainted dead away.

FOR AN INSTANT, he became transported in time. Flat on his back, just as he had been when he was twelve years old on Mrs. Chan's front lawn. From overhead, his angel descended toward him, as she had that day. Only, he wasn't on Mrs. Chan's front lawn, but on the carpet of his white-walled apartment, and the vision that lowered toward him was the woman of both his dreams and reality.

"Mr. Greeley. Are you okay?" The end tips of her blond hair lightly raked his cheek.

He fought the urge to pull her to him and taste those rose-petal lips. It took every ounce of willpower to resist the impulse.

"Yes," he said thickly, rising to his elbows, "just a little lightheaded. Serves me right for skipping dinner."

Touching his elbow with a sensual lightness, she helped him to his couch. On the white coffee table rested the platter with the banana bread. She lifted a slice and held it out to him. "Here. Eat something."

When he reached for the confection, his finger brushed hers, and a chill again ran up his arm.

As he chewed, she pulled a pen and scrap of paper from her pocket, and began to write. "This is my phone number," she said. "Call me if you need anything at all. Any time. Don't hesitate." Then, as a parting gift, she gave his shoulder a gentle squeeze.

He thanked her, and she left him in a daze.

Again and again, he played back the scene as it had transpired: the knock, the greeting, the fainting, the awakening; every touch, every word, every expression. *She had been in my home.* And she had left a trace of her scent behind.

How can I go on living like this?

He was on the third slice of banana bread when a thought struck him. An oily thought that bubbled up from some antediluvian sludge in his darkest recesses. *The book.* The other book. The one claiming to be written by the devil. The one the salesman had said was the book for which he had really come that day.

Pulling it from a bookshelf in his bedroom, he opened it and flipped through the pages until he came to the section labeled, "How To Get Someone To Love You."

"First, "the book advised, "you must get a strand of your subject's hair. Bind this to a strand of your hair."

Strand of her hair? How could he get that without drawing suspicion?

He read on: "Sprinkle on this a teaspoon of the spice from the flower of Crocus sativus, adding a pinch of orange zest."

A quick Google search informed him that the Crocus spice referred to was saffron. Of course, he already knew that zest was scrapings from the peel of an orange.

He continued: "Place these in a clay pot never used before. Mix in the earth from one of your subject's footprints. Now, fill the pot with soil and plant the seed of a black carnation. Water it. Then over the pot recite the spell, 'Dagon, goddess, born of the sea, Rise from the murky depths of your quay, Spring from the soil the fruit of this seed, And open to me the heart I so need.'"

Then, as the flower blooms and grows, so will your subject's love for you, the passage concludes. "But, whatever you do, don't allow any harm to come to the carnation."

How silly to think this ritual could garner Rowena's affection. And, yet.

He fantasized about his enchanted angel coming to him, kissing him, giving herself. The thought triggered in him ecstatic joy, and a tidal wave of lust that required his immediate attention.

The next day, he bought a tasteful planter, potting soil, and a packet of black carnation seeds from Harbo's Garden Center, wisely utilizing his employee discount. Then, watching carefully for the right opportunity, he scooped up soil left by the footprints of Rowena's Adidas sneakers in Harbo's parking lot. Finally, swinging by the Hy-Vee grocery store after work, he picked up saffron and a bag of oranges. Now, he had everything the spell required except the strand of hair.

How would a middle-aged man get a sample of a young woman's hair without appearing to be some kind of pervert?

As fate would have it, the very next day, a solution presented itself.

He was returning the platter on which Rowena had brought him the slices of banana bread when the door was opened by a skinny, pale, brunette woman with a wonky eye. "Yes?" she said. She held a pair of scissors.

"Is this Rowena Constance's residence?"

"It is. I'm her roommate, Wanda."

"I'm Andaman Greeley, from 305. I'm just returning this plate which she left at my apartment." He held it out to her.

"It's okay, Wanda. He's my boss," Rowena said from the other side of the door.

He stepped into what was obviously a space shared by women. On one wall hung a gallery of teal and fuchsia cartoon cats with soft, oversized eyes; on another, tiny, cubed shelves containing cherub figurines. Textured furniture filled the living-room area: a settee on a muted-pink throw rug, the lavender loveseat he'd spotted in the elevator the day she moved in, and a pair of moon-pod, bean-bag chairs. The delicate scent of potpourri permeated all.

Rowena sat at the kitchen table with a towel around her neck. "Mr. Greeley. Thanks for returning the plate. Wanda was just giving me a trim."

"You can call me Andaman," he said, approaching her nervously. On the table, on her shoulders and on the floor had settled feathery

159

snippets of golden-blond hair. It was all he could do to keep from salivating.

"Okay, Andaman," she said, melting him with her violet-blue eyes. "Glad to see you're feeling better."

"Yeah, well." He thought of nothing more to add to this, so attempting to prolong the conversation, he asked, "How do you like working with the stock group?"

"I liked the cashier register better, to be honest. Less lifting. But stocking is okay."

He froze. For a second, he thought she said "stalking" instead of "stocking." When he realized his mistake, he'd stopped still halfway across the room from her.

Wanda returned to trimming the back of Rowena's head. *Snippety-snip*. He tried thinking of some excuse to pocket a few strands, but nothing presented itself. *Snippety-snip*. Nothing that wouldn't appear licentious anyway. *Snippety-snip*. As it was, he already stood in danger of overstaying his welcome.

"Well, then, have a pleasant evening." He tried to make this sound as nonchalant as possible.

"You, too," she replied.

As he stepped out into the hallway, he cursed fortune for presenting and then denying him the remedy to his predicament.

That night in bed, he questioned whether he wasn't a fool for pursuing this madness. It was, after all, just superstitious nonsense. He had half a mind to throw out the pot, the soil, and the rest of his preparations. Whoever heard of such a thing? A love spell. Silliness.

But the yearning he felt for that sweet, sweet maiden, that was real, as foretold in a vision and in his dreams. Even now, just picturing her, a swoon came over him, and his heart ached.

He was almost asleep when he sat bolt upright. The solution to his difficulty was clear as a jewel: when they threw away the haircuttings, he'd just retrieve them from the garbage.

ANDAMAN LIVED ON THE THIRD FLOOR of the building, and Rowena lived on the second, but that didn't matter when it came to garbage collection. All the trash from the complex went down the same shoot and amassed in a dumpster below, where it was hauled away twice a week. On Mondays and Thursdays, if he recalled.

Of course, he would be at the mercy of timing. If the women disposed of the hair on the day of the garbage pickup, it would be gone by the time he returned from work. But if they threw it out any other time, he would be free to claim it.

He crossed his fingers.

The first night of his quest, a Friday, brought no luck. Rummaging through plastic bags of coffee grounds and eggshells and gawd-knows-what-all in the dead of night was about as unpleasant a task as he could imagine. Groping through the sticky, stinky, slimy detritus of neighbors and strangers made him gag, especially when he had to climb in among the bags to search through to the very bottom. By the time he finished, his clothes were sodden from head to toe. The smell of him was enough to chase off a skunk. Luckily, he ran into no one and gave himself a thorough scrubbing before heading for bed.

Saturday night was less unpleasant, since he'd already rooted through the dumpster's lower bags. Still, he came up empty.

Then on Sunday night, the night before garbage pickup, after having no luck on his first two attempts finding the sack with the hair, he tore open a white Hefty bag and out poured Rowena's pristine locks. Joy seized him. It was as if he'd found the pirate booty on Treasure Island or, more appropriately, Jason's golden fleece. Stuffing his pockets with handfuls of hair, he hurried back to his apartment.

ONCE HE PERFORMED THE CEREMONY, he covered the planter and its single seed with clear plastic wrap and set it on an end table where it would receive plenty of sunlight. All he could do now was endure the agony of waiting.

Sunday passed. Monday passed. Tuesday passed.

On Wednesday afternoon, he'd just overseen delivery of a hundred fifty-pound sacks of organic fertilizer to Harbo's greenhouse annex when he crossed paths with Rowena returning from her lunch break.

He steeled himself as best he could from the swell of emotions the bare sight of her unleashed in him. He tried to think of something to say to her, but all his thoughts derailed. *Come on, Andaman, use one of the bland salutations with which you greet the other employees.*

He started to open his mouth when she spoke first: "Afternoon, Mr. Greeley. You're looking sharp today."

Was that a compliment? He'd certainly take it as one. "Thank you, Rowena, but you really could call me Andaman. Most of the other workers do."

"Is that how you think of me? Like one of your other workers?" She batted her eyes shyly and tilted her head of shortened but still glorious blond hair.

He struggled to find an appropriate response. "Well … I … I, of course, value you for the unique contribution you make to your Harbo's team."

She frowned at him.

"That is, I look at you as a singular example of exemplary…"

Her frown deepened, and she extended her lower lip in an exaggerated pout.

This mannerism shattered his wall of decorum and he fought to maintain *some* propriety. At last, he said, "Your very presence makes my every day."

She smiled at him as if he'd just tossed her the keys to a new Lamborghini. Then she walked past him down the wide center aisle, and, unable to help himself, he turned to look after her.

When his workday ended, he hurried to his apartment and the pot in which he'd planted the seed. Peeling back the plastic covering, he gaped in amazement. A quarter-inch of green plant sprouted from the soil.

Was it coincidence that on the day this tiny plant began taking form, Rowena had, well, flirted with him?

He sat heavily on his ivory-white sofa, the planter still in his hands, and stared off in stark wonder. *Was the spell actually working?*

By Friday, at Harbo's, he had trouble concentrating on the simplest tasks. Luckily, the assistant day-crew manager—a calm young Black man named Dante Ridley, who wore dreadlocks, a nose ring, and, on his neck, a tattoo of a flaming skull—could be trusted with the routine running of operations, allowing Andaman to spend the bulk of his day hibernating behind the closed door of his office, fantasizing about Rowena.

Still, Andaman was the boss, and when a knock came on his door, he was dutybound to answer it.

The first interruption came at ten o'clock. Colleen Grimwood, his very pregnant cashier, stood on his threshold, clutching her belly and looking distinctly green around the gills.

"I'm sorry, Andaman," she said, "but I don't feel well and I have to go home."

Well, they could handle being down one cashier. They'd done it before on busier days. He nodded and motioned with his hand as if bestowing a blessing. "Go home, Colleen. Get some rest."

He was interrupted just two more times, once by Dante, who needed his signature on a delivery form, and once by a part-timer named Carol Bassett requesting a change to her work schedule. He handled these disturbances briskly and efficiently. The rest of the day was his alone. He spent it considering all things Rowena—her smile, her walk, her scent of peaches, the softness of the hand she'd touched him with on the night of the banana-bread fiasco, her stunning, violet-blue eyes, and radiant hair. He relived every moment he'd shared with her, often envisioning erotic alternative endings to these encounters.

When five o'clock rolled around, he was already in his gunmetal Toyota minivan, pulling out of the Harbo's parking lot, eager to check the growth progress of his black carnation. He'd managed to avoid his angel at work that day (for decorum's sake), but he hoped she would come to him tonight, or at least sometime this weekend.

He hadn't long to wait. No sooner was he in his apartment, gauging the development of his sprout, when a timid knock came to his door. He opened it.

Rowena, looking dazed and vulnerable, stepped into his arms.

THEY TALKED, kissed, ate, made love. Her, barely proficient in the tender arts, but soft and supple, and responding to his every touch. Him, the mature one, being patient with her, taking his time. Despite his girth, he performed with unimagined agility and grace. She brought out the sensualist in him. With her, he had the vitality of a tiger.

When he opened his eyes the next day, she was in his bed, curled up to him, her golden hair on his naked chest. He savored the moment.

When at last they arose, they showered and, still moist and pink-skinned from their shared bathing, made love again. They ate breakfast, then kissed and kissed.

It being a beautiful spring Saturday, they went for a walk, hand-in-hand, along 49th Avenue North, turned south on Quebec Avenue, and followed it to Sunnyside Park, where youngsters romped on a jungle gym and a pair of duffers in polo shirts and short pants took turns hacking at golf balls. The two lovers walked with the sun on their faces and rapture in their hearts.

Though scheduled to work that day, Rowena said nothing could tear her from his side. When they returned to the apartment, he made some entries on his home computer and awarded her an excused absence for the day.

All too quickly though, the weekend hours ran out and Monday rolled around with its grim reminder that they were still in monetary servitude to the great god Capitalism.

That day at Harbo's was excruciating. Every slow-ticking hour apart from her wedged a dagger deeper into his breast. Since Mondays were Dante's days off, Andaman's presence was required on the sales floor most of the day, addressing customer and employee concerns.

Twice, when Rowena passed him near the geraniums and, later, near the pruning saws, it took every ounce of willpower to keep from snatching her up and feeding, at least in some small part, the hunger she aroused in him. However, they'd vowed to keep their relationship a secret from their coworkers, even though doing so sorely tested their resolve.

Absent-minded and irritable, he nonetheless performed his managerial functions in a professional manner, until, mercifully, the clock struck five and freed him from his leash.

By six, they were back in one another's arms, kissing like schoolkids who'd newly discovered the wonders of love.

"I told Wanda she should start looking for another roommate," Rowena said.

"Another roommate?"

She eyed him slyly. "Since there's no place I'd rather be than here with you, big papa, I figured it would be simpler to just move in. I hope that's okay."

Move in? After just one weekend?

For an instant, he was dumbstruck. "Yes, of course. If you're sure. I'd be honored to have you here with me."

She smiled one of her patented, hundred-watt smiles. "Thank you, big papa. I feel so lucky to have found you."

With a sigh, she rested her head on the side of his neck and pulled him to her.

Their plan to keep their affair from Harbo's employees proved disastrously short-lived when, on Wednesday evening while dining outdoors at Namaste Café in Uptown Minneapolis, who should walk up to them but the enormously-pregnant Colleen Grimwood and her husband, Frank, a timid little man who Andaman found uncomfortably intense.

Colleen scowled at them in disbelief before self-awareness set in, and she offered up a flimsy grin. She whispered something to Frank, then they both approached her workmates' table.

"Hello, Andaman," she said. "Frank, you remember Andaman from Harbo's. Andaman's my manager. You met him at the Christmas party."

"Hello, Andaman," Frank said, extending a cold fish of a hand. Frank studied him as if he belonged to some alien species.

164

"And this is Rowena," Colleen said. "She works as a *stock clerk* at Harbo's." Her tone was almost accusatory.

The two couples exchanged awkward pleasantries before Colleen and Frank departed for their favorite Mexican restaurant. As they walked away, Colleen's gait took on a triumphant air.

"Well," Andaman said. "Looks like the cat's out of the bag, my dear. Tomorrow we'll be the hot topic of conversation. We'll probably face a dressing down from human resources and might even get fired."

"We can get jobs somewhere else if it comes to that," she said, patting his hand, lifting it, and bringing it to her cheek. Then she kissed his knuckles, and all his worries disappeared.

THURSDAY MORNING, they rode into work together in Andaman's Toyota minivan. They'd decided to hide their affection no longer. If Harbo's chose to fire them, so be it. They walked to the front door expecting the worst.

That day, as they anticipated, Colleen Grimwood shared the knowledge she gained in Uptown with all who had ears. The news trickled from one department to the next, eliciting the excited buzz fresh gossip carries. It even circulated in the warehouse, where he overheard a forklift driver whisper, "I hear the old man's boning that new blonde working in stock. You know? The hot one."

By five o'clock, the story breached the second shift and began spreading all the way to Harbo's sister store in Mankato.

Friday came and passed with no new developments. Occasionally, an employee stopped and gaped at Andaman from across the sales floor, and he knew Rowena received her share of unwanted attention, as well, but for most, the novelty of the affair began quickly wearing off.

By Monday, the grapevine was jumping with news of a coworker who spent the night in jail for smashing his car into a telephone pole while driving under the influence. On Tuesday, word spread that an assistant night-shift manager had quit to take a position with Harbo's dreaded arch nemesis, Bachman's. On Wednesday, the devil's radio tuned to a rumor that customer self-checkouts would soon replace regular cashier-operated registers at the store, which would result in wholesale layoffs. And by Friday, the pipeline flooded with accounts of the maintenance worker fired for attempting to pilfer a leaf blower.

By then, the hubbub stirred up by Andaman and Rowena's romance, though not completely gone, became fairly well muted. Although the relationship was clearly a policy violation, human resources never came knocking at Andaman's door. Apparently, no one had lodged a complaint, and no grievance meant no action, as far as the company was concerned.

What followed could only be described as the most glorious month in Andaman's life. He and his angel—winsome and perky and smelling like peaches—spent every free minute together. They took walks, went out for dinner, took day trips to Stillwater and Anoka. He even taught her to play chess, and though she still sometimes got the moves wrong and had no head for strategy, he still enjoyed playing with her. Regardless of what they did, his fondness for her never waned, nor hers for him.

They made love every single day.

Then, as it's apt to do, fate intervened.

On Tuesday afternoon, while a warm breeze drifted lazily through Harbo's greenhouse annex, a load on a forklift took an unfortunate shift and dropped more than two-thousand pounds of decorative cement paving onto the luscious blond head of Rowena Constance.

A LENGTHY PROCESSION of motorcars and pickup trucks wound from the church through the peaceful streets of Sleepy Eye to St. Mary's Cemetery. More than fifty people attended the interment. In the shade of conifers and Norway spruce, the stoic and the sobbing gathered around Rowena's coffin. Among those present were her parents, her siblings, her aunts and uncles, cousins, neighbors, and former classmates. And, of course, Andaman Greeley.

As the priest splashed the casket's bronze surface with holy water and said aloud the prayers for the dead, the assemblage mumbled appropriate refrains, and watched as the Earth slowly swallowed the metal box and its contents. The sight wrenched at Andaman, but he knew that he and his angel would not be parted for long.

In the wake of the terrible accident that had claimed Rowena's young life, all meaning had bled from Andaman's world. The only sensations that pricked through his layers of lethargy were bouts of irreconcilable pain. He stopped eating, stopped sleeping, stopped shaving, stopped going to work. He shuffled around his apartment with the now-withered black carnation he had used to first summon her love, pausing to sniff her clothing and her pillow, and remember with longing how she had all-too-briefly filled his arms.

He might have vanished forever in a sea of misery had a thought not occurred to him on the day before the funeral; a thought that instantly broke the spell of his deep depression and left him in a totally new frame of mind.

166

At her graveside, he slipped away before any in the crowd could ask who this ruddy-faced, mid-life mourner was. The family knew she was seeing someone from work, but they had never met him, nor had she described him. They certainly wouldn't have guessed this portly stranger was the one their Rowena called her papa bear.

Parked in the shade of evergreens, he watched as the others filed into their vehicles and drove back to the church, where a banquet of ham sandwiches and potato salad awaited in the basement all-purpose room. When the attendees were gone, a husky sexton rolled up her sleeves and went to work, spading soil back into the open grave. She toiled methodically, unceasingly, until the gap was filled to the brim. Then, she lit a cigarette and departed in a trail of smoke.

Throughout the day, other stragglers, alone or in small groups, gathered at various grave sites, read the tombstones, spoke to their dead. The universal story they told was of the pitiless wheel of life. Of the too-soon loss of loved ones and the knowledge that sometime, in the hours to come, other pilgrims will gather around the moldering bones of these mourners themselves and whisper the same empty words.

The day passed. Shadows lengthened. The sky went an unnerving copper-orange. Dusk fell, and still he waited.

Finally, in the dead of the night, he emerged from his minivan with a shovel and began upturning the still loose soil of Rowena's grave. He worked feverishly as if in a dream, coaxed on by the muffled encouragement of his sunken true love. *"Free me, papa bear. It's dark and lonely down here."* "I'm coming, dearest. Hold on."

Soaked in sweat, he worked the soil until, at last, metal scraped metal.

When he pried open her coffin lid in the moonlight, Rowena's face appeared, and he immediately understood why the family chose not to display her remains at the funeral home. Though the undertaker had made a valiant attempt to reassemble her crushed face, in the end, he'd come up short. Jagged scars showed through pancake makeup, and all her features appeared slightly off-kilter.

But the sight of her nonetheless lifted his spirits. "I've come for you, my dear sweet angel."

Her violet-blue eyes opened. She looked up at him lovingly and smiled, stretching out her hands to him. *"I knew you would, papa bear. I knew you would rescue me from the land of the dead."*

He bent to the casket and lifted her from the pillow and the overlay skirt. As he did so, the graveyard came alive with revenants, old and young, who stood at the plots of their entombments and silently witnessed him carry her off in the cool night air to his minivan.

Laying her tenderly across the backseat, he closed the door, started the vehicle, and headed to New Hope.

BACK HOME, it was just as it had been before.

They talked, kissed, ate, made love. For three days, they were inseparable. When the phone rang, they let it ring. When a knock came to the door, they ignored it. They weren't sure how long they'd have together, so they savored every minute.

On the hundred-mile drive from Sleepy Eye, they'd talked excitedly, like schoolgirls teasing each other about boys. What an adventure they were sharing!

When they arrived at New Hope, he'd borne her up the back steps, rolled in a carpet (just as he'd planned), shushing her when she started to giggle. Once inside the sanctity of their apartment, he unrolled the carpet and helped her change out of her grave clothes into a thigh-length kimono.

She felt to him as good as ever, though her flesh was cooler and less supple, and she'd taken on a somewhat waxen hue. Her features, of course, had shifted due to the wretched weight of the cement pavers that had collapsed her head. But otherwise, she was exactly the same. She even still smelled of peaches, though now with a mild industrial taint.

How comfortably they resumed their ways: returning to old patterns of speech, and to fond little customs of affection, such as him stroking her cheek with the back of his hand or her curling to his side in bed. Why couldn't they just be left alone in this love nest, drifting on the swells of passion? After all, who were they harming?

Sometimes he read to her from *The Merry Adventures of Robin Hood*. He told her about the trip to Lanesboro and the odd salesman and the book of spells. Or they listened to classic-rock tunes on the radio or played board games or assembled jigsaw puzzles.

At night, before turning in, they watched the TV news with the volume on low. On the second night, a story came on about a body stolen from a cemetery in Sleepy Eye. A news reel showed police milling about a gravesite bordered in caution tape. A photo of Rowena and her brilliant smile appeared next.

"Look, they're talking about you, my dear," he said, turning up the volume.

"... passing motorists reported suspicious activity. The next day, a cemetery worker told police that the grave had, indeed, been tampered with. An investigation revealed Constance's casket had been emptied, leaving her family and friends heartbroken. No motive was given for the crime, but Sleepy Eye police said they are pursuing active leads, and hope to resolve the case quickly."

The next day, a relentless pounding came to the apartment door.

"Andaman Greeley?" a harsh voice exclaimed. "This is the New Hope Police Department. Open up."

THE MEDIA COULDN'T GET ENOUGH of the story: The lovelorn garden-store manager who so adored his girlfriend that he refused to leave her side, even in death.

Reporters from as far away as Boston and Portland, Oregon, joined in what could only be described as the circus atmosphere of the People Versus Andaman Greely. Updates appeared nightly along with photos of Andaman in shackles being led in and out of the courtroom, and live interviews with police, attorneys, and others connected with the case became newscast staples. Every day, a crowd of rapt observers arrived in hopes of getting a seat at the trial. Those who didn't, contented themselves with gathering outside the courthouse, many wearing T-shirts with photos of Andaman, and boldfaced captions that read "Endless Love" and "Undying Devotion." Others waved "Free Andaman" signs or passed out petitions calling for his release.

Of course, most people were appalled by the affair, digging up corpses not being the sort of thing folks did in civilized society. But throughout the spectacle of the trial, while the pro-Andaman people were out in force, the majority kept their silence.

In the end, Andaman was sentence to the St. Peter Regional Treatment Center for an indeterminate period. Speaking at his sentencing hearing, he simply asked the judge: "Can I have Rowena back now?"

For seven years, Andaman received treatment for his delusions. Slowly, the ground built back under him and, at last, he gave voice to an understanding that the dead are gone for good and deserve to rest undisturbed. The doctors all remarked on what outstanding progress he had made, and wrote glowing reports. Then he was released to a halfway house in Minneapolis where, eventually, he was allowed to occasionally wander unsupervised.

A Bachman's in Bloomington hired him part-time as part of a state program that encouraged businesses to hire the handicapped. He worked stocking plants and plant food, and was well-liked by his workmates. When asked about his past, he'd always say, "I was just so in love with Rowena, I'm afraid it affected my judgment."

Did he regret it?

Here he'd sometimes get teary-eyed. "I regret putting my friends and her family through it all."

Eventually, Bachman's hired him full-time. He moved from the halfway house to an apartment just across the parking lot from where he worked. He met a widow at Bachman's named Mable McCain, a sensible, age-appropriate companion with a full-grown daughter. Soon, he was living with Mable in her home near Highland Lake Park Reserve.

Life with Mable settled into an easy routine. Few highs, fewer lows. When he went to bed at night, he knew exactly how the next morning would unwind: from the wail of the alarm clock to dressing in the clothes Mabel laid out for him to the cereal he'd have for his breakfast. Typically, it was Wheaties or Cheerios.

On their days off, they'd attend church choir performances at St. Alfonzo's in New Hope or stroll the pond and grab a bite to eat at Centennial Lakes Park in Edina or play bingo at a neighboring senior center.

Every night, they'd turn in at nine o'clock. Sometimes they even made love, though not usually. In either case, they were sound asleep by ten-thirty, without fail.

Andaman seemed content with this schedule, though sometimes Mabel caught him staring wistfully in the distance and wondered what was on his mind.

Then, one day, he proposed.

"No sense living in sin," he said lightheartedly.

She, of course, accepted.

In coming days, Andaman grew more quiet and withdrawn. Mabel attributed this to the fact that, despite being in his fifties, he had never before married.

"A change like that would give any man pause to think," she told her daughter.

On the day before their wedding, Mable sent him in his rattly old gunmetal Toyota minivan to the store to buy some lightbulbs for the kitchen. One hour turned to two, then two to three, and still no Andaman. Where could he have gone? She tried calling him on his cellphone, but her calls all went to voicemail.

Was he in an accident? It wasn't like him to lose track of time this way.

She went out to the garage, snooping for clues. Things out there looked the same as always. She poked around the snowblower and the lawnmower, studied the tools he'd left out on his workbench, examined looped extension cords, Christmas decorations, storage bins.

Mabel was about to leave, when something odd caught her eye. A shiver ran through her.

In a corner, among the gardening utensils, lay an empty space where one of the tools was missing. That tool being: a shovel.

Acknowledgments

People ask me where I get the ideas for these stories. The truth is, for me, it's kind of like making vegetable soup. The carrots, let's say, are a remembrance of something I experienced in a dream. The cauliflower may be something I saw on the television news. The onions are part of a story I read on an internet site. The celery is a reimagining of a snippet from a classic tale. The potatoes come from things witnessed in everyday life, though usually twisted into another shape. And the rutabagas (and most of my stories tend to be rich in rutabagas) gurgle up from some murky sludge in my subconscious. I mix these ingredients together in my writer's cauldron and, hopefully, something spooky emerges.

Oh, yeah, and being a dedicated reader is essential.

Sometimes people tell me things that get my imagination going.

For instance, Debbie and I were at a concert in Maple Grove, Minnesota, when my friend Karen Lashbrook sat down next to me and told me about a dream she'd had years ago when she went through a divorce. In the dream, she kept finding pieces of her ex around the house: limbs, fingers, legs, and so on. Bits of him stuck around even after they'd split. I could not let go of this imagery and, with her permission, her dream became my story "Leftovers," embellished, of course, with details from that murky place I spoke of earlier. Thanks for sharing your dream with me, Karen.

Thanks also to Jennifer Thompson, my eagle-eyed (step)daughter, whose talents as a proofreader have saved my butt from an embarrassing mistake on more than one occasion.

Also, thank you to my wife, Debbie, for being Debbie. Thanks to all the people who have encouraged me in my writing quest, especially my aunt, Carol West, and author, editor and blogger M. Grant Kellermeyer. Thank you to all the readers who have taken the time to review one of my books, even if they panned it (because, hey, at least they read it).

If you enjoyed *Echoes From a Shoreless Void*, consider recommending it to your neighbors and friends on social media. Also, reader reviews are the lifeblood of modern publishing, and posting a brief review on Amazon, Goodreads or your favorite readers' blog would help a struggling author immeasurably.

For updates on my work, and other readings on dark fiction, check out my website at: www.joepawlowskiauthor.com. You can follow me on Facebook @ Joe Pawlowski, Author or on Instagram @ joepawlowskiauthor.

Let the Terror Continue

OTHER BOOKS BY JOE PAWLOWSKI

In the Heart of the Garden Is a Tomb

Nine nerve-tingling tales of the weird, the supernatural and the bizarre. Three friends lost on backwoods logging trails stumble on an ancient graveyard where a monster sentry from long ago await. A woman who struggles with a terrible loss finds she can only save her sanity by taking drastic action. A retiree, empowered by a gun found in his garbage can, learns that becoming a man of action isn't all it's cracked up to be.

These and other lost souls are only seeking a way out of their dire circumstances. But there's no escaping the bitter truth that awaits us all in the heart of the garden.

Available from Amazon in paperback and ebook. Free on Kindle Unlimited.

Why All the Skulls Are Grinning

A shaken teenage girl, lost and abandoned at the gateway to another realm. A man driven mad by isolation who believes he's built an automaton to lead him back to open skies. A car salesman whose girlfriend winds up a sacrificial offering to a rock god's dark deity. The stories contained in Why All the Skulls Are Grinning look into these tortured lives and many others.

Why are all the skulls grinning? Could it be because they have to smile to keep from shrieking?

Available from Amazon in paperback and ebook. Free on Kindle Unlimited.

The Cannibal Gardener

A gardener with a secret life, a Goth woman with a morbid fascination, a serial killer who leaves a trail of bodies across the

Midwest: they all come together at a Minnesota lakehouse in a transformation as evil as it is shocking.

The Cannibal Gardener combines out-of-this-world horror with a love story and a touch of grim humor from a master storyteller.

Available from Amazon in paperback and ebook, and on audiobook from Amazon, Audible and iTunes. Free on Kindle Unlimited.

The Vermilion Book of the Macabre

From author of *The Cannibal Gardener* and *Dark House of Dreams* comes this highly anticipated collection of 16 spellbinding tales of supernatural suspense.

Readers call it "a blood-chilling collection" and say of Pawlowski "he paints his dark tales so realistically you will have nightmares."

Available from Amazon in paperback and ebook. Free on Kindle Unlimited.

The Watchful Dead

A 12-year-old boy housebound all his life, a conjure woman who speaks to the dead, an evil slave trader driven ruthless by greed and a war hero whose greatest battles take place in his own mind: all are about to have their lives shaken to the core by powerful forces from beyond the grave.

Readers are calling it "a ride right off the bat" and "nicely written, with a lyrical quality that kept me turning virtual pages," and the author "possesses the talents of a classic great writer."

The Horror Review says *The Watchful Dead* is "a gutsy, ambitious, skillful exploration of cosmic/epic dark fantasy."

Available from Amazon in paperback and ebook. Free on Kindle Unlimited.

Dark House of Dreams

In a city overrun by ghosts, fear lurks around every corner.

Add a murder plot, a devastating earthquake, a missing mother, a gang of outrageous villains, and a young boy tormented by demons both real and imagined, and you have an epic quest through the hidden places of monsters and gods.

Readers say it's a "well-written and creepy" journey that begins with a secret revealed in a charnel cave and ends with a hard-earned lesson learned in a *Dark House of Dreams*.

Available from Amazon in paperback and ebook. Free on Kindle Unlimited.

Made in the USA
Monee, IL
12 May 2025

17213546R00105